WALK AWAY

A hapless victim trapped in an abusive, loveless marriage decides to flee and save herself before it is too late.

A novel by

Anitha Padanattil

RG
books

books

Published By

Redgrab Books Pvt. Ltd.

942, Mutthiganj, Prayagraj, 211003

www.redgrabbooks.com

contact@redgrabbooks.com

Price in india : 200/- INR

First published by Redgrab Books in 2022

Copyright © 2022 Redgrab Books Pvt. Ltd.

Copyright Text © 2022 Anitha Padanattil-

Printed and bound in India

Cover Design & Typesetting by Redgrab Books team

ISBN : 978-93-90944-85-9

Acknowledgement

My thanks to author Neelim Akash Kashyap for being a pillar of support and Pinak Pani Basistha for the intial look through.

I am also grateful to all my reader friends and family for being consistently supportive. Know that you are in my heart forever

PART I

Fanciful thoughts are dreams
That hover on delicate wings
Over the course of a day.

Wayward flights that rise
And bank steeply
Reining in the drifting clouds.

Choked nuances scorched
By desires that ebb and turn
Through tunnels of shallowness.

Webbed in intricate clumsiness
Stroked into feverish submission
An ache that streaked through -

Like veins beneath skin
Nothingness could bloom.
Regress or waft - works both ways.

Innocence does not lie...
Does not last
Hence, slow-build on the colors.

Feed on the beauty
before they fade
And turn into nothingness.

***

Happiness was a farfetched thing thought Mala as she scrubbed at the pots and the blackened frying pans heaped inside the kitchen sink. Why, it was only yesterday that her husband Prasad, who had been offered the job of a peon at her employer's office had the temerity to not turn up this morning at the appointed hour. He must have pawned off his b**ls to have his regular fix, she thought in fury. What was she to tell the saheb? How would she face malkin? Her phone rang twice and she understood that it was them even before the call was picked up.

They had been patient with her and listened to her litanies in sympathy. She had received financial help from them whenever the need arose. Her family was indebted to them forever. But the man in her life? The drunken sloth she was tied to?

The very thought made her insides tremble in grief. She was cheated of a life and opportunities that were never to come. Chained to a future that had systematically nipped away at her childhood. Tender years that came equipped with a burden so heavy and had never been in the reckoning. Who was she to blame?

It was her fate. Her wretched karma that led her to live like a bhikari* begging from flat to flat. A routine that began at four in the morning and ended at six in the evening. A ladle flew from her soapy hands and landed on the tiled floor with a tinny clang. Mala jumped at the sound but it helped shake her out of her reverie.

The kitchen door opened softly and her mistress, Monika looked in. With a soft smile, she enquired, "Everything fine? Nothing broken I hope?" Mala picked up the ladle and smilingly assured her malkin that all was well. Satisfied, Monika went back to the front room. The Yoga channel on the TV was running. Mala could hear the muted sounds of Chitti Swami's soft chants. Monika madam was a follower of the Guru. One among the millions around the world that revered the Guruji*. Mala hurriedly touched her forehead and the base of her neck to convey her reverence to the Great One. She was just a sapling on the ground. One, that could be trampled upon by anyone, anytime. She did not need animosity from any quarters least of all the Guru and his followers. What if he could divine her thoughts? Monika madam might throw her out. Her family would be cursed. Her man could rot away for all she

Walk Away

cared but her three children? They were her lifesavers. The reason for her existence. How could she wipe away their future?

Appeasement of the Gods was a carefully cultivated trait and was instilled in all of them from a tender age. The fervency was in direct proportion to the increase in despair, feelings of insecurity, thwarted ambition, rigorous and punitive devotion but never pure love. Guruji was part of the same divine, it was her reasoning. And so, she would try to rein in her thoughts and hope that she would be paid several lacs of rupees for being true to her faith someday. Her thoughts bloomed with an oversized image of the great man. If he did read minds, he would understand the supreme effort that was required to remain steadfast and not stray towards the lesser-known so-called godmen. Most of the upcoming ones she knew were trying their best to carve a name for themselves and lure innocent followers that would ensure an invincible stature.

Perhaps they were as good or even better than Pujya* Chitti Swamiji* himself. But subscribing to each and everyone's channel on the internet was a tough thing to do. Who had the time to listen to their long-drawn sermons? One was enough. They could focus better and continue to live their lives in the manner they were accustomed to. The Pujyavar made few demands unlike the new ones who read out lengthy, itemized lists of ingredients required for auspicious ceremonies and events. These went on for almost all the days of the week and unless your pockets were loaded, you would befall a terrible fate.

The phone rang again and Mala's musings stopped as abruptly as it had begun. She turned towards the jhadoo* that was placed behind the door and began to sweep the floor. The TV had been switched off. Monika madamji has completed her session. She would walk in and begin her preparation for breakfast. Good thing. She sorely needed a cup of tea to reinvigorate herself. Food could wait.

Mala completed sweeping the kitchen floor and carefully gathered all the bits of hair and dust into the dust-pan. After tapping it into the garbage bin, she moved to the spacious living room. The sun had just risen and it looked to be the start of a beautiful day.

Floor length windows opened out into a lush terrace that spanned the city when one moved in for a closer look. Watching the sky from within the plush interior always gave Mala's heart a sense of thrill. This was the reason she opted for the early morning session at Monika madamji's house. That, plus the delicious Mangalorean breakfast she got to have everyday suited her sensibilities perfectly.

She has turned into a true-blue city dweller having arrived here a decade ago. The farmlands she has cherished in her childhood have been relegated to a significant part of her memory. Although she yearned to have a glimpse of her old parents, it was their casual dismissal of her youth to a life condemned to domesticity that pained her the most. 'Bonded laborer' was what she called herself in private. Anyway, that was what she was. Her upbringing had never allowed her to throw away a relationship that had shackled her. Born, brought up, given away, mercilessly used and now, guardian and provider of a family of five. Mala's actions were automatic as she swept under the sofas, the ottoman, past the potted plants, dusted the carpets and moved steadily towards the glass fronted view. Birds chirruped outside, busy in their multitude and her glance skimmed over the tiny hopping bodies. A burgeoning sparrow population was indicative of a thriving upsurge. In her village, they represented fertility and happiness. However, their arrival meant that the harvest had to be protected as well. All the young ones would turn into live scarecrows, running through the golden fields, whooping and creating a ruckus that would prove an effective deterrent against the flock of invaders. Mala remembered her kurti that tore mightily as one particularly sharp frond caught on the faded cotton and refused to let go. Oh, how she had felt low and chastened after the incident. She smiled grimly--- as she recalled the look of horror on her mother's face and how she had been locked in her room for a day as punishment.

The screeches of the morning visitors intensified forcing Mala to stop the flow of thoughts and move towards the large TV placed on the oblong shaped table. She began to wipe the screen gently, often tilting her head on one side to view the vanishing streaks and the remaining fine dust that had to be cleared.

Numerous figurines of the Buddha adorned the space adjacent to the television. A separate wall fixture was dedicated to effigies of the elephant Lord Ganesha and variations of the portly silhouette graced this space. A giant urn filled to the brim with water on which an LED tealight floated that was sometimes surrounded by perfumed roses or the mildly pungent yellow marigold added an old worldly charm to this corner.

Malkin* had a keen eye for aesthetics that calmed one's mind and supervised the decor of her home to ensure that it always looked crisp and spotless. It was like looking into the pages of the Chabi Chaap - the weekly regional magazine that she pored over without fail. The homes that were pictured inside could have easily been that of her Monika malkin.

By now, Mala was wiping the glass windows and looking through them at the deep blue sky. Wisps of cloud floated by lazily and she thought she spotted a horse's head amongst them. Busy hands soon stilled and the dreamy expression came into being once again.

Chamanbad in Bariched Taluk. Her hometown. Where kites flew high up and she would sit on the verandah of her house watching them hover and flutter like giant-colored butterflies. Her eyes would follow their gentle movements as they flirted with one other. When a colored square of paper dipped, the other would follow. On and on went their strange dance, as they steadily climbed the vast horizon. Higher and higher would they twist and turn. Those patches of blue, red, green and yellow.

"I want one maa," she managed to whisper in her mother's ear as she expertly plaiting her oiled hair and tied the ends using colored string. As she pulled at it with a quick sharp tug, Mala hissed in pain. "You are not a boy to be playing such games. Once I'm done with you, sweep the courtyard and draw water from the well. Your father and brothers will be here soon and they will need to wash and refresh themselves." And Mala would mutely comply with her mother's order. Just the same way she acceded to all the demands put forth by her father and brothers. Bitterness at the unfairness of it all would plague her but she would tamp them down just as quickly as they rose up. She was no different from the others she knew. Yet, the injustice of it all shrieked out its presence and every time Mala heard the catcalls, she would inwardly flush in despair.

She longed to fly kites. And run blindly. Lift her heavy skirt and show her ankles as she ran. She wanted to laugh out loud whenever she felt like it. When fat Raju fell from his bicycle. When a passing crow squirted its ash-colored paste on her brother's shirt. When her roti had a weird shape instead of round. Why was it so wrong for her mother or her aunt to laugh out loud? Why did everything have to be staid and painfully serious? Wasn't the earth happy at their existence? When they would eventually disappear, would the smiles return? Mala wondered at this but received no answers to her queries. Not that anyone heard them anyway.

She never saw the insides of a classroom but she was not unlettered. How could that be, you would wonder. Well, Mala spied on her brothers when they loudly read out their lessons while she went about her tasks and unbeknownst to them, their fervency fed on her curiosity. Soon enough, Mala found that she could read slowly, one letter at a time. The process was arduous but she stuck to it until she felt that she was fairly proficient. After that, there was no looking back. In everybody's view, Mala was illiterate and therefore, her thumbprint was of value but the girl knew better. She would outsmart everyone when the time was right. She would make her future count and not spend the rest of it in obscurity, enslaved and deprived. For the moment though, she chose to lie low and allow the dingy cloak to envelope her like all the girls of her taluk. Nameless shadows that merged and flitted about and that suited everyone just fine.

***

Veneers were omnipresent. They tied themselves to everything that could be conceived. Thoughts, words, life... anything and everything could turn out to be the proverbial package waiting to open up.

When it was considered appropriate for Rashmika to get hitched, the search had begun in earnest. After all, what could be more proficient for a physiotherapist with a plum job at the Astrid Hospital in Karwar than an engineer or someone with a similar qualification? The horoscopes that piled in were like a constant flow. They came packaged in all things bright and beautiful. IAS officers, IPS officers, entrepreneurs, engineers, pilots, men with cushy central government jobs, doctors - a never ending stream of eligible bachelors hoping to join the bandwagon of the happily ever-after.

The thrill of working in a well-known organization had its own benefits. You met well known faces. Heard their personal stories. Listened without comment and offered no opinions. That was the rule. To be the silent listener. It was tragic. To know that what was presented to the world was not the real deal. Both differed. The variations were wide. Like ensembles worn for the stage. The preparation that went into creating the façade was mind boggling. Often, the inner persona would try to claw its way out but the layers had to be firm you see. Those could not change. The outer could not crumble. Because those were the things that were perceived. Those were the very least that was expected of you, from you.

So basically, the discovery that every individual has two sides to their personalities with the one that remained hidden, being the real deal was a given. Yet the dormant one was quite potent. Passivity had a strange effect after a while. It tends to creep in slowly and subdue the dominance. Layers are built up and strengthened. The clinging on continues long after the need diminishes.

Stark memories crept in and remained. They were the accompaniments. Like a second skin. A presence that is conjoined. A weird conversation with a notable personality was suddenly remembered and the mood plummeted. It was a dark, depressing day. Not surprisingly, it also was the onset of the monsoon season.

The rains beat against the walls. Hammered against the windows. Rattled and drummed on the roof in an incessant pattern. It was cold and the humidity made us shiver. All of us in our uniforms suppressed the tremors and rubbed ineffectually at skin exposed to the elements.

Madam Renuka, wife of a prominent politician joined me (Ms. Rashmika R, BPT) in my room for her fifteen-minute session. She obediently took the gown that was offered and went behind the partition to change. I gestured for her to lie face-down and she climbed up the stool and did exactly that. Madame has IVDP - Intervertebral disc prolapse that required seven continuous days of treatment.

I folded the sleeves of my coat and flexed my arms and hands. It would be a tiring session I knew. The patient had rolls of fat covering her body. Her hips and buttocks were dimpled on account of the deposited cellulose and I observed her spine structure intently. I had my work cut out.

Squeezing out some gel into my hands, I applied it on her back. The gel was cold and she flinched. The electrical modality, in this case the ultrasound, was to be used for fifteen minutes to stimulate the pressure points. I adjusted my grip on the handle of the sensor and began to run it lightly down her back. Restore and correct - that was to be the feature of this session. After a few minutes, she settled down and began to relax. As her shoulders began to slump, I knew that a rapid snooze mode would follow. But, to my utter surprise, the opposite happened.

"You have a magical touch Sister."

"Thank you. I hope you are comfortable. If you feel any discomfort, please let me know," was my polite rejoinder.

"Hmm. Alright."

A few minutes passed by. Madame R fidgeted. I waited for the next one.

"You are too pretty to be doing this job."

I offered a noncommittal grunt in response. This was a common enough query and one, that I considered to be a disadvantage. The field was demanding enough without having to fend off the unwanted attention.

"So. Why?"

Curiosity killed the cat, that's why.

Speaking out aloud was an effort but she wouldn't back down and I fidgeted in uneasiness, before continuing, "The field of medicine interested me. My grades didn't qualify for an entry into areas that required specialization and this was the next best thing to be in."

"But, but," spluttered the lady in indignation. "Surely there are other fields that you could excel in. Modeling, journalism, airline stewardess

                    Walk Away

and a host of other glamorous fields that you could get into even now should you fancy it!”

“I’m sure Madame. But the thing is, those things never interested me enough. My preference for the medical field has in fact, brought me here.” I felt that my placid response incensed her. I hoped she would shut up but alas, it was not meant to be.

“Such a waste of talent and beauty.” I could hear her mutter. I suppressed a quick chuckle. Another ten minutes to go before she would be on her way.

To deflect her from probing further, I countered with a question of my own.

“Madame, your husband must be concerned about you. About your condition I mean. Has he accompanied you today?”

A brief silence fell upon us. I looked at her legs. My glance swept over the upper thigh to the calf muscles, her ankles and finally, her feet. They were shiny and smooth. Baby pink lacquered toenails complemented the well-heeled look. The props were acquired at a great price to keep the look intact. The resplendent one that was projected to the world at large.

Madame Renuka cleared her throat. I knew she had made up her mind, “Oh him? He lives in his own world. The new one that he created. It’s a pretty one you know. Somewhat like you.”

My hands stilled for a second. It was as though they had divined the response in advance. Madame continued, oblivious to the split-second reaction, “It is good that he did not turn up today. You would have caught his fancy and then he will try his best to create yet another world for himself. Much like the Kings of yore you see? Men who live to conquer worlds. Large hearted men.” The dispassionate condescension stung. It was aimed at all men of course. At their largesse. They set about creating man-worlds within man-worlds. The system suited their fancy. Perception blurred within realms of reality versus fantasy.

Sympathy for her invaded our silence. It was a momentary introspection, each to their own sort of thing.

I heard her sniff. It dejected me. I knew she had children. Her body told me that. They would be well looked after. Or not!

My eyes were on the clock. The fifteen minutes elapsed. I didn't want to be rude though.

"They are sycophants. Every one of them. They offer what he needs and takes what he can give."

I had to end the session. We are taught to be firm. Firm and polite. So, I gently placed the sensor on a small table. The hint was broad enough for her to rise from the prone position. Holding onto my gaze she continued, "You seem to have made a wise decision Sister. I should hand you that. Your camouflage is perfect." I smiled at her gently and assisted her in stepping down from the high bed.

"I have a post though - an unofficial yet, important one. You can get in touch with me if you require help in any way." I inclined my head and folded my hands in a namaste. Madame Renuka went behind the partition once again and came out after a few minutes resplendent in a colorful silk sari. Her aloof persona was back in place. She swished past me with a curt nod.

The hospital gown had stripped her of her identity, I realized. She swept away her public face and laid bare, the persona that was hers alone. For a brief moment, I had been a witness to the despair. That shriveled interior that carried on for the sake of several reasons. Their children, the identity, status in society, material benefits and a host of other reasons. So, wasn't she as good a sycophant as her better half or for that matter, the 'others' that co-existed alongside her snug little world? Had she tried to dismiss the air of nonchalance by bragging and complaining incessantly? She seemed to choose to wrap herself in such a way that her reality would seem like a single-layered entity to others.

My contemplation had to stop else, my work would suffer. And so, I turned towards the bed to deftly peel away the disposable paper sheet and replace it with a fresh one. Washing my hands was next after which, I sat behind my desktop to type in my observation. My next patient would pop along soon.

***

Sahaj waited anxiously to have a glimpse of his beloved. His little bird, the physiotherapist was lodged in the other wing of the hospital and he was here, ensconced within the administrative wing.

Drab, drab life.

How he ached to tear out of the oppressive walls and fly out to keep an eye on his almond-eyed beauty. It was her milky-white skin and direct gaze that had floored him. For here in Karwar, the girls were demure and looked respectfully downwards when a male gaze settled on them. The upbringing was so fierce that were emotional bonds to develop, they would be cruelly hacked at and dismembered even before the wings sprouted. So, when the newcomer walked in past him as he casually lounged by the reception chatting with the old-timers of the days shift, he was caught off-guard. The feeling was like a punch in the gut. For a minute, he looked on at her receding back in bemusement wondering what the hell had just happened.

Rashi in the meantime, had already entered the lift, unaware of the turbulence she had created. She was rushing to meet the Doctor in charge and take up her assigned position as Senior Physiotherapist at the said department.

It was a week later that she began to note an eager set of hands helping her with her bags or getting her a place in the lift. The person, she noted was average looking and generally pretended to be unaware of her presence. A sidelong glance would however confirm that he was blatantly staring at her profile. When caught in the act, he would blush a deep beetroot red.

Rashi was amused by her 'invisible' knight in armor. After all, she needed a diversion from the mad routine. She was new to the place and needed friends. But the attention seemed unwelcome after a while. Flowers and chocolates began to line the therapy room. She became the butt of jokes and her male colleagues waspishly commented that she should satisfy her craving with romps in the utility room. Would he be satisfied if she gave in, was what she wanted to know and her barbs hit the mark. The comments dwindled after that. Jokes could fall apart. If one was lucky enough to hit the jackpot, a good ending could be hoped for but she was not ready to take the risk.

The next day would find her inspecting a few of the wisecrackers nursing cut lips and mild bruise marks. So, she thought to herself, her invisible bodyguard was turning aggressive. That was not a good sign. Perhaps he would develop into a stalker as well? Already her PG hostel mates reported seeing him loitering by the hostel gates late in the evening. It was as though he had taken up the unofficial post of looking out for her. Lord save her. She definitely did not need a shadow at her beck and call. The work excited her but the rest could wait. How was she to convey that to him without breaking his heart?

It was maddening to not be able to come out of her room and stand on the balcony facing the road. He would be waiting there like a lovelorn hero aching to have a glimpse of his pretty heroine. Rubbish. She hated the melodrama. It irritated her no end. She wished she cold spout the choicest of cuss words and drive him away. Her upbringing did not allow her to vent out in this manner. It upset her to hurt someone intentionally that way. She couldn't converse in Kannada or Konkani either. How was she to let him know that she was not the kind of girl he needed. She wanted her freedom. Being away from her conservative parents gave her happiness. The thought of 'Hitler' being here every weekend to keep an eye on her made the bile rise up her throat. This was sheer bliss; her present life. Except for the sour taste that rose in her when she spied him lurking in corners looking for no, spying on her; she was having it all her way.

It was worrisome too. For although this was a picturesque town, she knew no one here. There were no guardians she could cling on to, no friends she could confide in. Perhaps her Hitler could provide some protection after all? That evening, she dialed Mandy's number.

"Hey, it's me. You free?"

"Hi girl. Where have you been hiding? Still cooped up under Hitler's wings I suppose?" The laughter that followed was painful to the listener. Along its concise beats ran episodes of embarrassment. Rashi cringed and laughed weakly. She wished that 'Hitler' was here with her though. She had deeply resented his presence at one point of time but he had been pivotal in her quest towards independence. How could she not acknowledge that?

                                                          Walk Away

'Hitler, Hitler…'
That incessant chant
Meant to provoke, tease and taunt.
Meddler and proverbial third eye
Ramakrishnan Kurup. That was him
Her father.
Lone warrior. Commando.
Fierce Ninja with the gaze that shot daggers of
steel. Hands that spanned yards
Spoke of loyalty
Ones that thwarted impudence.
Lashed out - to make short work of the defiant,
Tongued wrath that subdued the fiercest of spirit
Father. Protector. Pillar of strength.
Unassuming granite wall and, cradle of love.

"Whoops. Having trouble, are you? It's too bad we are not with you. You would have welcomed his presence now that you are free of us, right?"

Mandy was sharp. Her acute sense of understanding brought in a fresh spurt of tears.

Inhaling she exclaimed irritably, "Well, why don't you give the poor guy what he wants? It will cure you of your homesickness too. And you will finally know how good it is to spend time this way. High time you dropped the pavitra savitri* act. Dive in and enjoy the ride. You are not so young anymore and moreover, no one will know, if that's what you are thinking."

She was bold, brash and, right as always. I had to concede.

The Punjabi strain in her lent the extra fillip. She knew how to live life queen-size. Live, eat, bang around, smoke like a chulha and drink like nobody's business. I learnt to enjoy my pegs from her. She taught me the finer points and encouraged me to be refined in my tastes. As far as the rest was concerned, I begged to differ.

She sounded composed. It seemed that family life with a second kid that was soon to come had calmed her down. Hopefully she had shrugged off her inclination towards the occasional joint. Clouds of smoke notwithstanding, the real Mandeep Kaur would rise before us. Our laughter riot session creator. She would grin and snort, mumble incoherently, try and flash her assets, and pretend to be horny and ride on one of us. Clumsy actions that made us roar in laughter. The same one who was offering what according to her, was a practical solution. It was a good one. Her suggestion. But I was not cut out for that. Hitler had brought me up too well. Demure, practical, staid as a nun and respectful to boot. The Malayali groom who would wed me would have been blessed thousand-fold in his previous birth. For in his hands would be given Rashi - veritable human angel from the household of the respectable Kurups. Untouched, pure as a newly bloomed blossom and highly qualified with a career that was just beginning to burgeon.

We reminisced and spoke for a while. I ended the call and sighed. That had not been helpful. Perhaps Pranauti could help me out. I would call her tomorrow.

***

I opened the rusty gate at the back of our building and made a quick turn towards a nearby lane in case the 'invisible' stalker caught me in the act. This was getting to me. The cat-and-mouse game I mean. I couldn't run from this situation any more than was required. If Pranauti would not offer something feasible, I would have to ape Hitler's moves. The new avatar could prove to be a shocker and Sahaj might be in for a rude surprise. I hated thinking along this line.

My phone rang and I fished it out of my bag. "Yes ma?"

"Molu, are you on your way to the hospital?"

"Yes. Another ten minutes and I will be there. Why? Anything urgent?"

"No, no." There was a brief pause. Ma pausing to gather herself before the onslaught. This was better than the caning I use to get from her when young. Living up to the expectation of being the class topper year after year, proved to be exhausting. Although my grades were

Walk Away

better than bad, they were definitely not better than the best and trying to achieve that perfect ten proved to be a herculean task. I began to detest the load that was placed on my slim shoulders and began slipping down the grade list. The beatings were in direct proportion to the dipping of the scores. From being the apple of my parent's eye, I turned truant, renouncing decent conversations with my mother for a long, long time. I found that I hated her with every ounce of my being. My brother, who arrived after a good eight years, was pampered and cossetted like a miniature version of God himself. He gleefully absorbed the adulation and, would observe me with that sly, knowing look. It rankled, that look and I itched to wipe that smirk off his face. Every time the memory surfaced... the queer churn in the pit of my stomach would make its presence felt.

Hitler on the other hand, was not the guy with the brawn at that point of time. He reserved his affection for his little princess and indulged her (yours truly) with the choicest of goodies. I have reserved a special little place in my heart for the man even though he developed this bothersome behavior that led to the development of the unfortunate moniker and subsequent clashes which I shall mention in a while. He was only being protective I knew. NO father would want his daughter to succumb to the lure of the devil and with two irresponsible chattels (poor Mandy and Pranauti were considered to be the epitome of the said term) holed up with his precious, all he could do was to rush over in the direction of the students hostel after work every single weekend, and take charge. Sadly, I seem to have lookouts like him popping up every now and then even though I am advancing in age. Although I reassured myself that the case isn't so with my reflection in the mirror staying true to form, fact is fact. I am deeply entrenched into what I term as 'the active biological phase' and time could soon pass by leaving me in the lurch. I take great pains to nurture my physical self and that pleases me to no end. My current aim is to maintain the form I am blessed with and when I enter the realm of domestic bliss, I shall have the last laugh. Things will change, never fear - I keep telling myself.

My thoughts prove to be prophetic, I realized later. But by then, it was too late to turn tail and retrace the path that had been traversed.

Maa's shrill voice rang in my ears and I roused myself from

the thoughts I was immersed in. I was an expert at blocking out her instructions. The ones issued at rapid fire pace. Those days were behind me in any case. But wait, she was talking about a cousin of mine who got engaged. The boy was residing in a fancy town in the city of Paris. Lyon - it was called. Cousin Bhama was planning to give up her plum job at IBM and take off for the quaintly named place soon after the wedding. Better to latch on and start a family right away, she was heard saying. Bhama was past twenty-five and plump to boot. Being rotund was considered a deterrent when you were scouting around for a life partner. It would be fine once the kids arrived and the family rhythm was settled. Her career could be taken up after that or they could plan

Aunt Maya was waiting for Bhama to leave their home. It would be a relief. The pressures of having an unmarried daughter at home was unbearable. It was embarrassing to explain to everyone that the girl's horoscope was messed up as in, royally complicated and that she had to be married off to a fully-grown plantain (tree) before the regular rituals were to be observed. Something about warding off the evil influences of certain planets that cropped up in the horoscope.

Rashi barked out a laugh at the thought. Bhama was quite cross at the thought but resigned. She was eager to flee the shenanigans that the elders came up with, and live in a place far, far away where she would be left unbothered by such ridiculous sentiments.

"Your horoscope has matched with a few eligible young men. I want you here this weekend. Let's start the process. Probably both Bhama and you could complete your ceremonies within days of each other."

Rude awakening. My thoughts trailed to a stop.

I was stunned!

And that was how Sahaj found me, slap bang in the middle of the busy road, hanging on to my phone, jaw wide open in disbelief. I vaguely recall being maneuvered to the side of the road having narrowly avoided a head on collision with a honking van.

"What is that noise Rashi? Are you crossing the road?" yelled maa.

I deposited myself on the sidewalk, unable to reply, unaware that I had been guided to safety while my shield blocked me from the irate passers-by who had witnessed the near-catastrophic event.

I managed to mumble out a response and end the call. The tirade would continue, I knew. Mum didn't enjoy being crossed. She would harangue me on my lack of etiquette and absentmindedness. Call me out until I apologized. That, I would deal with later.

I was finally being used to cast the bait.

I would be the lure.

Just when I was climbing the career graph.

I didn't want to end up like the other cousins of the family. Meek, subservient, with erased memories of the past whose existence depended only on the present. Poor Bhama. She would end up that way too. I felt a pang in my heart.

What was the use of the education I slogged for only to have it thrown away into a sea of nothingness? I would not oblige. Mr. Ramakrishnan has to accede to my request. Although maa stopped with the canings ages ago, her words still held us captive. Eons ago, I imagined witnessing the lights of our home flickering in fear unless she willed it. Perhaps that was just me. My eyesight could have dimmed for a second. Momentary panic does that to you. I know that now.

Sharada was the only child. A rarity in those days. She was born with a rare condition called - Atrial Septal defect. A hole in the heart was explained as being congenital in nature; treatment involved complex procedures and was best left as is. So Sharada - my mother, basically grew up with everyone around acceding to her wishes and treating her with deference. For someone who was supposed to have a low life expectancy, maa went on to live a fruitful life until she was sixty-five.

It believed that the multifarious Gods stayed by her side. They were the silent sentinels who ensured that Sharada lived her life well. In turn, her devotion towards all of them lined up inside her altar was so fierce that she would spend a minimum of four to six hours cloistered within their midst. To her, they mattered the most which was followed by her pet peeve; family.

It was she who chose Ramakrishnan as partner in the forever game. It was in deference to her condition that both groom and the family agreed to the union. Her first cousin was also aware of the benefits of being passive and that kept the peace between the two until the time she passed away. So basically, the family life of the house of the Kurups floated along quite placidly but after Sharada's exit, diplomacy found itself being abandoned and in its place came into being, a crusty old curmudgeon.

Salient points being; difficult to handle, sour faced with an acid tongue to boot and a temper to match. Gone were the days of diffidence. Had it always been there? Veiled until the wind blew it away. People grew and shed skins throughout their lives. Perhaps the invisible layers were extensions of the same thing. You grew, relearnt, discarded previous notions, formed new ones, checked them for fit, draped around and went on with life until it was time to begin all over again. That had to be the real deal I suppose.

Life was quite like that. A long unwinding road that lay ahead; filled with cracks, bumps and potholes. You learned to avoid the pebbles, sidestep that ditch, slow down and go easy on the speed breaker and finally pace on once everything seemed smooth and easy going. You have to watch out for hurricanes that come your way, swerve when an obstacle looms right before you, and hurry up ahead before your time is all but spent till you find exhaustion settling its tentacles on you.

Speaking of exhaustion well, here I was, sitting listless on the footpath by the side of the road while all these thoughts crowded up into my head. I am late for work and Mr. Hopeful has taken it upon himself to be my beatific angel. The heat of the sun is flashing on my face and I squint up at him blinded by the light.

Not bad.

This then, was Sahaj. I realized that I never actually looked at the man. His eagerness was the only emotion my antenna had honed onto. His dressing sense though, was appalling. And those shoes. Where did he pick them up from? They were horrendous. Well, what else could you expect from a man who was bred in a town that pretended to call itself a city? I wrinkled my nose in annoyance.

Rising up from where I was stationed, I began to walk in the direction of the hospital. Sahaj accompanied me and held on to my elbow as though to offer assistance. The cheek. I shook my hand in impatience. His crestfallen expression was almost comical to watch.

I had to warn him to reign in. I was not the romantic kind. Never had been. No fascination for that kind of thing. Nope. No.

Pranauti… you better come up with something to save his sorry ass. Else I might have to whack some sense in him and God forbid, were that to happen. For I did not want to turn into the very avatar I hated since my childhood days. I did not want to become my maa. Sahaj, you pathetic dullard, for pity's sake, please try and get this through your thick skin that you do not interest me. Not now. Not ever.

My head buzzed busily as I chastised myself. I refused to turn into a veritable do-gooder. The one with the humanitarian streak whose heart dripped in concern and oozed sympathy for all earthly beings. My heart was firmly in place and my head needed sorting out.

And thus, we walked in silence towards our common destination-the town center, where proudly stood the tall edifice, Astrid hospital, opposite the Karwar fire station. Work beckoned.

***

The sun never looked happier.

It was a hot day no doubt but that did not deter the little girl prancing by the roadside to look up at the bright sky. She walked for a while and reveled in the freedom. Her mum had asked her to collect a sachet of milk from her aunt. And she grabbed the chance before her mother had a change of heart. Nine-year-old Rashmika was unused to walking under the midday sun. Once the initial euphoria settled, the downturn made its appearance. Flashes of light popped behind eyelids and colors danced before her vision. Then happiness turned dark. Her sandaled feet came to an abrupt halt and a set of soft white hands rose up involuntarily, to cover the uneasiness. Worry took over in an instant and a sheen of sweat marked the once clear forehead. Little Rashmika felt her legs give way. And as she dropped to the ground, all she thought of was the feel of the sun on her body. Her pretty white dress would be ruined too. How her mum would thrash her for that. Soon, darkness enveloped her and she settled within its folds.

The loud thud grabbed the attention of the passersby and the child was lifted and carried by concerned citizens to the neighboring bus stop that had a pretty little sunshade. It was apparent that Silverton Biscuits had kindly sponsored the red and white striped canvas awning. The letters were painted in giant letters on the front and offered a decent shade from the sweltering heat. Clucking noises of concern were made and someone offered to sprinkle a palmful of water onto the girls face. Once Rashmika was revived, she was offered a mouthful of water and gently asked about her place of stay. And thus, ended the girl's sojourn, her first, on the back of a bicycle. She was dropped off and received a string of the choicest of epithets for the unremarkable achievement. Her mother had an acid tongue. The disappointment of not getting the sachet of milk in time for her to prepare the day's sweet dish left her fuming. The bright white dress with its prominent patch of red mud on one side and a faint tear along the seam incensed her too. How she rued her decision. The girl was incompetent. She should have asked her husband to fetch the packet rather than cave in to the child's pleas. Today's lunch would be a sad affair. Her face flushed in shame as the image of the kind samaritan dropping Rashi back home mere minutes after the trip had actually begun, rose before her.

After instructing the child to drop the dress outside the door before she washed herself thoroughly, Sharada picked it up with a sigh and walked towards the handpump by the side of their house. Only a thorough scrubbing under the rush of water would remove the dirt following which, it would have to be soaked in soap water. She hoped to be able to rescue the dress. The hand-me-down was literally a gift from the Gods. Her distant cousin was kind enough to hand it to her since her daughter had outgrown it. Her fingers trembled as she caressed the soft material. Oh, her Rashmika had looked like an angel in it. The frothy white layers of lace had highlighted her childish features and added to the charm. The problem with her girl stemmed from her being overly sensitive, thought the disgruntled mother as she scrubbed at the stain. Rashi's skin would turn red after a few minutes under the sun and peel away leaving her looking like an overripe cashew fruit. She had also begun to day dream of late and had to be forced to complete her lessons. Sharada detested having to nag. It drained her out. The fact that she suffered from a congenital ailment of the heart meant that life was handing out to her the opportunity of a lifetime, section-by-section. All her actions therefore, were premediated. Her choosing of a husband, her opting to work as a teacher in a school that offered a moderate schedule, the saving of every penny that they earned into a nest egg meant to secure their future and relying on her mother's pension for their daily expenses. She had a practical nature and logical mind. Emotions were considered as secondary. Her father had been recognized as a freedom fighter years before he passed away and now, her mother received a sizeable income that could meet the needs of their family. Not that the mother minded. Her Sharada could never go wrong. If her daughter felt secure and happy, she would be at peace.

Her medical condition terrified her parents enough to stop having more children and so, everything that they possessed, was essentially hers. Sharada did not turn out to be greedy or spoilt. The credit for her upbringing went to her parents. She grew up well aware of her frailties and yet, desired a family. One that would be at her beck and call. Her silent prayers asked for a life that allowed her just about time to ensure that her children were well settled and content. She figured that her Rashi might have need of familial support apart from the man in her life and hence, she strove to produce a male child - eight years after her daughter's birth.

The boy was the apple of her eye just as much as her Rashi but the girl did not understand it yet. All her beatings went in vain for the child failed to achieve distinction in her studies. Without being the school topper, there was minimal chance of her being accepted into a medical school and hence she would now have to make an alternate plan and scrimp some more to ensure that Plan B fell in place a few years from now. The change in plan played havoc on the worried mother's mind. Her son was cautious and attuned to her moods and therefore applied himself to his studies rather well. Such a bundle of joy he was, she smiled inwardly, satisfied.

There was the additional stress of having to look far more affluent than they were in reality. Care was always taken to ensure that Rashi was always clothed in garments that seemed upper class. They did not need the country bumpkin looks.

Her husband had a comfy job in the Railways and hence, they were assured of annual first-class tickets to a destination of their choice within the country. So, the touring and sight-seeing part was covered. Both she and her husband would benefit from a fat payout and pension at the end of their service and they would not need to depend on their children to take care of them. So essentially, Sharada was practical, shrewd, and yes, quite sharp. Her functionality covered them in a protective blanket and so far, she had things figured that kept them going. Her instincts told her that the soft skills she displayed, would be imbibed by her children. As for her core skills? Well, she believed that they would be put to use someday.

Until that happened, she would have to wait. Muttering angrily, she rubbed the fabric between her fingers unhappy in the knowledge that the stains were here to stay.

***

Chitti Swami's session had considerably improved Monika madam's moods. Mala thought happily of the piping hot breakfast she would be served as a direct result of it. The besan or gram flour had been sieved and placed in a shallow basin on the kitchen countertop. She hoped that madam would make the Mangalorean version of the besan cheela with chutney and tamatar wali sabzi. That, plus a cup of piping hot tea would bring the strength back into her bones. Mala could hear madam humming. Another good sign!

Beaming in happiness, she walked over to the balcony and stood watching the plants and flowers.

Do butterflies fly this high? A small brown and yellow flecked butterfly moved busily from flower to flower. The roses smelt good too. Mala walked over to the jasmine plant that had bunches of the sweet-smelling flower waiting to be plucked. She touched them lovingly and took a single flower that was placed at the side of her bun. Madam did not allow for the blooms to be plucked and yet filled her home with bouquets that were purchased from Julian's - the flower shop that had recently opened on the ground floor of their apartment. Both Namita,

Walk Away

the owner of Julian's and Monika madam shared a common love towards plants that flowered and they often exchanged useful tips over the phone.

Mala began sweeping the balcony and gathered the soil, fallen leaves, scattered hair balls and the occasional bits of paper and dumped them in the compost bin kept for the purpose. The refuse reeked of rot. Scraps from the kitchen found their way into the bin as well and the slurry was used for production of the plump vegetables that were used in the same kitchen. It was a strange cycle but one she could relate to.

Both her family and their ancestors were people of the soil and offered the earth what they received in kind from her. Had she been the recipient of their understanding and received a minimum of five years of freedom, she would have done her bit to improve their lives. Instead, here she was, dependent on the kindness of her employers to be able to run her life. Granted, she was lucky. The earnings from her work were enough to maintain a roof over their heads and keep food on the table. But what would she do if there was a sudden calamity? A natural catastrophe like the floods that ravaged other states? Where would she and her little children go? How could she ensure their safety until they turned independent, were the thoughts that ate at her every time. Mala's actions stilled unknowingly. She stood absorbed, statue-like, pensive and absentmindedly tapped at her broom with a free hand when the call sounded from inside. Rousing herself, she walked in and closed the balcony doors. The house was cool and pleasant as she walked on in the direction of the kitchen. Something was cooking and her nose lifted in anticipation.

Picking up her plate and cup from the side rack, she sat cross legged on the floor and looked up at Monika with an eager smile. Madam took three crisp cheelas from the casserole and placed them on Mala's plate. Next, she spooned the chutney and the tamatar sabji beside it and watched Mala dig in hungrily. The cup was topped with her special brew while she continued to flip a few more cheelas. Mala was famished. She had left home early without having a drop of water. Monika sensed her mood and tossed in two more of the lentil pancakes. Mala continued to eat without pause and managed a grateful smile at her kind-hearted employer. To Mala's knowledge, no other lady of the house served their bai* a freshly cooked breakfast with such devotion every morning.

Monika waited patiently for Mala to finish eating. They could speak as she sipped on her tea. As for herself, it would take a while for her system to rouse itself. She had downed a liter of warm water in the morning and that had to be flushed away... before the cheelas could enter. Breakfast did not entice her as much as the yoga session and her precious plants and she went through the routine just to make sure that poor Mala ate heartily. The woman had three hungry mouths to feed plus her wastrel of a husband. The woman worked hard to keep them clothed and well fed and for her to stay hale and healthy, she needed to be well-nourished as well. Giving her a hot meal, once every day, was the least she could do to help out.

As Mala relaxed her back against the wall with a sigh and sipped her tea, Monika watched her and smiled.

"Feel better now?"

"Yes. So much better. Seriously, you are such a good cook madam."

"Naah. I'm not into cooking. Besides I don't need to cook full time. There is no need for that, is there?"

Mala went quiet at this. Monika madam and Pritam sirji were childless. Madam hailed from a coastal town in Mangalore and Pritamji was a Punjabi. They worked together for a while until their friendship had blossomed into love. Mala knew that madam had turned to yoga in a bid to stabilize her mood swings. Of late, she seemed disheartened. Sirji spent his time in office and there seemed to be a lack of communication between the two. It was sad really.

Could a miscarriage bring about the death of a friendship? After all, it was not a fault really. Things happen for a reason. Madam had broken down in front of her on two different occasions and Mala felt sad for her. Here was someone who had everything and yet, yearned to have the one thing she had thrice over. Mala comforted the weeping woman by saying that the two were young. They could continue trying after a while. But the couple were drifting apart and Mala worried about her job. She did not want to lose it. She prayed to Matoshri* for the two to get back on track soon. Life would be easier that way. Selfish motives often require focused goal setting. And Mala was quite clear in

                                                   Walk Away

her thoughts that way. She had to adopt a cautious approach.

"There is still time madamji. All you need is hope. Do not let go of that. In our village, our elders remind us every time; once hope is lost, everything is lost."

Monika looked towards the balcony absently. Mala knew that she was paying attention and so, she persisted. "There is a time for everything. Even for the children to be born into this world. For the one you lost, perhaps the time was not right. Once you are ready, everything will fall in place. Both you and sirji are a wonderful couple." At Monika's quick glance, she continued, "Look at us - so not made for each other, the imperfect Jodi that's loaded with three young ones. Such an irony, right?"

Monika barked out a short laugh and Mala joined in with her trademark deprecatory smile. Presently, she arose and walked over to the kitchen sink to wash her plate and cup. After placing them upturned on the rack to allow them to drain, she wiped her hands on her sari pallav and turned to look at her employer. Woman met woman squarely in the eye.

"Get sirji home as often as you can madamji. Speak to him, reminisce about the days you spent laughing whilst in each other's arms. Cook him all his favorite foods, allow him to touch you, bring magic into this home, your plants, your life. You will thank me then."

Monika's eyes welled and she spread out her hands helplessly. Words formed within her but she was choked with emotion. The damn woman was right. She needed to get her act up and going. Pritam was uneasy in her presence. Before she antagonized him further, she had to tidy herself up.

"What other advice do you have for me, maharaniji*?" she enquired of Mala in a teasing tone.

Mala laughed sheepishly at that and hefted the mop and bucket. "Beginning this weekend, plan A is to be put into action. Rest for later," she concluded with a smile.

Monika let Mala be and carried her breakfast to the balcony where she sat thoughtfully and pondered over how the weekend could be effectively tackled. She needed her man. It had been a long time and

Pritam had better be prepared.

Mala in the meantime, swept through her duties at Apartment number 315 with a happy heart. If things worked out here, she would be genuinely happy for the couple. They were genuine human beings and deserved all the happiness they could get. This house needed to hear a baby gurgle and coo. It needed to be turned into a home.

***

Ramakrishna Kurup packed his bags and slid off the counter behind the reservation booth at the Railways office - central depot, Thiruvananthapuram. His shift was over for the day. Precisely at five p.m. he would walk out of his workplace, climb the fifty odd steps that curved and led down to platform number One. Negotiating through the crowds and the assorted stalls selling food packets, beverages, confectionary and books, he would walk past the waiting rooms and the numerous red shirted baggage handlers, towards the main gate where he would nod a greeting to the black coated individual who kept a lookout for persons entering the giant entrance. The queue was heavy this evening and Ramakrishnan stood in line watching people get their passes inspected and punched by Sohail. A police constable stood at the opposite end and keenly watched the outgoing crowd. People jostled past each other with some accompanied by scrawny children and others loaded and cramped by assorted baggage, harried employees making a beeline towards the exit. There were small-time vendors clenching empty baskets, wheelchair ensconced individuals being pushed by helpers or family members and the constant moving sea of arms and legs made for an unceasing influx, like a giant tide that swelled and rose. The constable was methodical in his approach as was the official ticket checker. Steely eyed and trained to pick out the shifty eyed and suspicious, the few that were hauled, were handed over to the Railway Patrol counter which was a small booth below the stairway for further cross questioning. Many a times, it would be an irate customer who didn't match up or a loudly protesting repeat offender who would try to trick or duck through the invisible barrier that the duo had set up.

It almost never worked though. The government officials had scanners that could see through your persona. Years of experience had honed their capabilities to near perfection. Ramakrishnan watched all this dispassionately as his body inched forward like an automaton.

Once he moved past the gate, the steps that led outside were cleared and he hurried towards the corner where the employees parked their vehicles. Abdu stood up from his rickety stool and gave him a half-hearted salute. Ramakrishnan acknowledged him with a smile and mounted his scooter.

He drove at a sedate forty mph towards his Pallikal home. A restful three-bedroom house built on five cents of prime ground within the city. The breeze washed over him as he navigated between the honking cars and speeding buses. The buses had to be avoided. They were the musth ravaged elephants of the road. Anything living or otherwise would be plowed through with little consequence and one was better off safeguarding one's own resources as no mercy could be expected if the fate that befell a person was of the extreme kind.

His Sharada would be waiting for him. A cup of hot tea and some homemade snacks would be placed on the dining table covered by an upturned saucer and plate. She would be in the backyard ripping off poor Mala, their house-help who was stuck around for six to seven odd years. It was a miracle that the woman tolerated his wife. Very few could. He was one among the lot who did and knew that he was ridiculed for it. His son adored her. But his Rashi, she was the exact antithesis of her brother. The girl practically detested Sharada. He could see it in her eyes. Although she practiced silence and never remarked on anything with an ounce of enthusiasm, he knew that his advocating on behalf of the mother would come to naught. Sharada ruled their household with an iron hand. She has been his cousin. It has been a calculative plan. Their marriage. He had been selected and toyed with. Although he had not seen it coming, by the time he had known what had hit him, it was too late.

Ramakrishnan honked impatiently just outside the closed gates and the little imp - Sanal came running out of the house followed by his sister. They whooped and came to his side in a rush. He allowed them to hop behind him and off they chugged on inside. This was a routine that was followed since Rashi was little. Taking his bag, the girl sprinted inside and he went into their bedroom to wash and change. Afterwards, he sat on the table and quietly sipped his tea and munched on the snacks. Sanal joined him and they amicably shared the snacks. Once done, the boy rushed away to play on one-half of the gate, swinging back and forth while its hinges creaked in symphony. It often put his teeth on edge but Sharada let the boy be and he did not want to overrule her. For that matter, he did not override her on any important matter that pertained to the house.

Where was his sweetheart Rashi, he wondered? Probably poring away at her books, he thought glumly. That had been the single and only bone of contention between Sharada and himself. They had violent disagreements whenever he broached the topic in private.

"Leave her alone. Let her be. Can't you see the shine die away from her eyes? She is so young to be shut in. Let her play. DO NOT force her Sharada," he would entreat but to no avail. Sharada remained firm.

"You do not understand. Our girl is a weakling. She needs to be tough. And academics will save her at some point of time. She cannot be left behind. Just cannot," countered his wife in bitterness.

"But she hates you. She understands that there is a difference between your treatment of Sanal and her. That is wrong. Pamper her dear. Only mothers know how. Only you can bring the light back into her eyes."

"Oh, don't I know that?" was her angry retort. "But frankly I do not care. The world thrives on inequality. She has to learn to withstand that. When I am gone, do you think her father or her brother would be there for her? She has to learn to stand on her own feet and survive. That is the greatest gift I am giving her. I am training her to throw away her vulnerabilities. Let her continue to hate her mother. That will make her angry enough to stay strong."

And Ramakrishnan could not counter-argue beyond that. Sharada used her most potent weapon. A limited lifespan. One that could be snuffed out anytime, any day, any instant. He lived with that knife pointing at him since he married her. The children did not know. They didn't plan on telling them as yet. In a way, his hands were tied. With a resigned sigh, he gave in and she enfolded him within her arms.

The first time he actually noticed her was when they were all grouped together to play touch-me-not. They were a vivacious group of cousins and as they prepared to begin running from the one who was meant to give them the 'touch' Sharada appeared from the house, silently seated on the topmost step of the row of stairs leading to her home and watch them with a laugh. She looked pretty he remembered. Quite demure and fair with two long plaits hanging down her back. She was pretty and, quiet. One of her key traits - observation, stemmed from her silence. As they played, she smiled and watched them run as though possessed by the devil. When he was nominated to do the honors, she watched in delight as the fleet footed escaped his clutches. Once, their not-too-agile cousin named Gowri stumbled and tripped over a small pebble thereby losing her balance and hitting the ground with a dull thwack. The result was a bleeding lower lip. He remembered stopping the game and calling out for Cousin Mukundan to help carry Gowri into the house. Sharada came and opened the door wide enough so that they could carry the bitterly sobbing girl inside. Cousin Raman ran to the fridge and returned with a few ice cubes wrapped in a handkerchief to be pressed against the girl's throbbing lip. Sharada took the pack and placed it at intervals while her free hand rubbed the girl's back as if in comfort. Ramakrishnan remembered their eyes meet in mutual understanding.

She had been an only child. The family was aware of her condition and the fact that she was delicate in nature. Her mother - their aunt, had this desolate air about her at all times and the children were all asked to treat the cousin with a high degree of sensitivity. They often overheard their grandmother berate the poor lady as to why she had desisted from adding to her brood. But Sharada's parents were stoic and firm in their decision. They would raise their child as best as they could and leave the rest in God's hands. She was provided a good education, lived long enough to be allowed to work and marry the man of her choice.

It was said that Sharada was reared with a gigantic advantage when compared to the rest of the cousins. The choicest food, best clothes, the convent school that the rest hungered to attend, the lack of taunts in her case compared to the remonstrations the group received in abundance.... in short, she lived like a little princess and went on to live life her way, on her terms. Everything that she achieved in life was closely monitored; approved decisions that she knew would offer her an advantage over others.

Although envious of her good fortune, most sympathized with her unfortunate situation. For someone who knew that life held her on a leash that could snap anytime, Sharada seemed pretty oblivious to her fate. She always seemed placid and when a few sneaked looks at her, it was as though she was unaware of what ran through their minds. Ultimately, it was Sharada who had laughed her way to the altar - with a man who did not know what had hit him. He has been strung like a puppet and taken through the preplanned rituals much like a tame bear dancing to his master's tune. Ramakrishnan's account of his life went this way:

'It was in the year 1972 that I completed my B.Com from the SriVarma college before going on to write several exams that would secure me a job at any of the government banks or institutions. I envisioned myself to be leading a stress free and comfortable life. In those days, working in a state-owned establishment or a central government workplace was like being offered manna from the heavens. Your life was secure, the family ecstatic and your life after completion of the allotted work term would be cushioned from the handouts passed on by the said organization until the time, you departed for the afterworld. So basically, I was considered the savior of the household.

Since father was a small-time shop owner and the family's expenses were mounting, I was asked to take a loan to meet the wedding expense of my younger sisters. I was pacing along comfortably despite the financial encumbrances when the next bombshell struck! The elders huddled together and decided, practically demanded that I should marry Sharada and give her some semblance of a life.

Now, sympathy and living out a life were two different things. I had my eyes fixed on a pretty young intern from my department. The office was awash with the gossip too. Two lovebirds in the throes of a blossoming romance. My colleagues were avid watchers and waited to see how events would shape up. This then, was a spanner in the works. Veni would be crushed. I was crushed too. How on earth could I disappoint Sharada. She has a weak heart for heaven's sake. To top that was the embarrassment of having to marry a cousin that I knew from the time I was little. Why didn't she refuse for heaven's sake? Was she being coerced by her parents as well? How did I not see this coming?

I lamented on my luck taking a downturn and my friend Shankar agreed ruefully. Veni heard of the latest development and sobbed in her corner for the whole day. None dared comfort her. What could anyone tell her that would offer relief? She was just turning twenty-one and the emotions of the young are material for high-octane potboilers. They surge and heave at random and leave a frothy wake upon their passing. Two days went by in this manner and I was asked to stand up for my rights. I needed to be more assertive. I was not the cornered woman for heaven's sake.

Yet, a distant part of my being reared its sentimental head. Sharada was not strong, physically. That she has a mind of steel, I would discover later. If she has set her heart on marrying me, wouldn't I be breaking her heart? One that was already damaged? That would be the gravest of sins I would be committing. Abandoning a helpless, challenged soul towards an early grave. Surely, she was not at fault here.'

I was to offer her a helping hand, argued my father. She has a good enough job. She was not siting idle at home, twiddling her fingers like most would, given her condition. In addition to this, the thought that her high-and-mighty cousin could back out anytime seemed to be fine with her. She was such a sweet thing, really.

The last statement gave me some hope. Father could speak to her right away and confirm her suspicions to be true.

'Unfortunately, I will have to pass up on that offer my son. You, will have do the decent thing. Speak to her and let her know that you like someone else from your office. That would comfort her a lot.' The sarcasm was meant to hurt and it did. I told them about Veni and how she has given her heart to me and the information started off round two of an acrimonious session.

'Our son has become a mini-Krishna. Caught between the fancies of two women. One, that he has known since childhood and the other, that is young, flirty and prepared to take over.' My mother was silent in the face of the barbs spewed by father. She perceived my moral dilemma. I wanted a cushy life now that my responsibilities were dwindling. Veni and I could earn a comfortable sum together and live a settled life.

With Sharada, the reverse would happen. My responsibilities would double. I had to cushion a drama queen for life. There were no guarantees that I would have a wife after a while. Or children for that matter. Veni would be long gone by the time I reverted to my single status. So, was the happiness that I deserved being handed on a platter? It seemed to me that I was to be the sacrificial lamb at the altar of everyone's happiness.

The next bug that bit me was about my transferrable job. How would my wife, Sharada travel to all the places I was stationed in? How would she adjust to all the different locations? What if she fell ill all of a sudden and the place we were in, did not have the kind of medical facility that was required? Incessant thoughts crawled through me all day long. I lacked concentration at work and Veni stayed away from the office. She had applied for a week's leave. Her empty station bothered me. Life was miserable and I hated my family and the others who watched me knew well what my answer would be.

November 11th 1975 was the day I joined my wife in wedded bliss. The day was bright and not a speck of cloud marred the clear sky. My cousins were ecstatic and my parents were triumphant. All the elderly uncles and aunts were supremely happy and, relieved. My sisters were crestfallen and I shared the sentiment. I was a bundle of nerves not knowing where I was headed.

As for Sharada, well, she had her placid expression in place. When our eyes met, I discerned her smile. It had a victorious tinge to it. The bait had been cast and the snare tightened. I realized then that this had been her plan all along. Sharada had judged me quite rightly and had placed her bets on the winning horse. Only, the gambler and the bet were both made by the same person. It has been Sharada who stage managed all of us, the bumbling fools into this moment. And she had found herself the perfect stud to steer her to victory - a good-natured oaf named Ramakrishna Kurup!'

***

 Walk Away

Mala was furious. She was being supervised. Eagle eyes sat beside her and watched as she struggled with the shell of a slippery mussel. There was a basketful of the mollusks that had to have their shells pried open and the minute flesh scooped and deveined. The task at hand was strenuous and being probed by 'the radar' did not make it easier. Mala paused for a second to wipe her face on the sleeve of her blouse and resumed the task. There was another kilo of fresh sardines left to clean after which the household cleaning jobs had to be completed. It was a pain to have the lady of the house take an active interest in something she had no knowledge of. Madam was a vegetarian but she cooked for the family with a zeal that left Mala amazed. Granted, the lady was Shoorpanakha* personified but to cook something for the family that she had never ever tasted, coupled with managing the affairs of the household and an active day job meant that she struggled to keep up with the herculean nature of her duties. Mala had on occasions, seen the madam gasping for breath and leaning against the countertop for support. She would rouse herself after a while and walk on towards the dining area to assemble everyone for their night meal. It was a miracle how she kept a hold on things considering the fact that she had to also contend with the resentment that her daughter nurtured against her. Oh yes, Mala knew that only too well. Madam knew it too and cared two hoots. For the moment though, everything was hunky dory. But there would come a time when she will have to reach out. By then hopefully, Rashi would rally around. For whatever reason, the mother was bent on waging an ongoing battle with her silent yet determined daughter. And the mother's rage would be vented in part against her poor self. Mala grazed her thumb and stuck out her tongue in pain. Her day dreaming would end in trouble one of these days.

"What happened, have you cut yourself?" asked Sharada madam worriedly. She had discerned Mala's sudden intake of breath.

"It's nothing amma. Such things are part and parcel of life. What is one nick when there is a husband who has nicked you for life?" Mala immediately regretted the words the moment they were uttered. After a short silence, madam began abruptly, "You can stop cleaning the fishes. Just drain the water and store them in the fridge. I shall cook something else tonight."

"No, no amma. I shall complete this right away. But promise me that you will give me a portion of your delicious fish curry and mussel dry fry. The children love the food you cook and we shall all have a feast tonight," she added cheekily.

"I always do that. What is special about today Mala? Don't go all sweet and sugary with me. You know I detest that stuff," was Sharada amma's abrupt retort.

Chastened, Mala set about completing her task. It was true, she thought as she absently rubbed her thumb. Sharada madam had a kind heart. It alternated between the cast iron wrapped avatar and the melt in the mouth gooey one. Mala carried home a portion of the dinner cooked here without fail. Every evening, she was given a packed set of dabbas containing a freshly cooked meal that thankfully spared her from the drudgery of cooking at home. Her family survived on this outpouring of generosity from the day she began working here. It was precisely this reason that stopped her from quitting. Abstaining from work also meant that the nightly ration would disappear and that was unacceptable. So, she grit her teeth and foraged on.

How on earth was one able to cook something that seemed abhorrent to their very nature, mused Mala. Pure vegetarians' shudder at the thought of a meal that contains the flesh of animals; basically, anything that strays from the vegetable kingdom. So how did Madam get to this point? A deep love for the family - she rationalized. After all, which other factor could motivate a woman other that this? It was like a tide that consumed. Gnawed and ate at you, through you. But you would not dare give it up as this was the foundation that sustained you. Women have this invisible core that gives them the strength they require when in need. Their radar is on high alert at all times and when an incoming tide approaches, they face it with equanimity. Do or die. This is how a woman is created. Mala, Monika, Sharada - one woman, many names. Scores of them. Countless faces. But dare the unseen advance and even death would be defied.

Mala smiled in happiness at the turn her thoughts had taken and piled up the deveined mussels on a plate. She rose up on her haunches and climbed the steps to walk into the kitchen. Handing over the plate to Sharada madam who was busy slicing onions and green chilies, she walked out once again. The sardines had to be tackled and her mouth watered at the thought of the dinner they would all be enjoying tonight.

Mala began cleaning the fishes of their scales and gut. As her hands busied themselves, she looked up at the neighboring tall edifice that towered over the house. The sixteen storied apartment had been a detached bungalow just like this one but the owners had passed away a decade ago and the property had been given away for a staggering sum to the developers who proceeded to demolish it and construct a high-rise in its place. Mala imagined Monika madam looking down at her from her bedroom window of the tenth floor. She smiled at the image and half waved, knife in hand. Convinced that she was being watched and had been offered a wave in return, Mala smilingly resumed her task.

Monika and Sharada madam were friends. They had common friends and common interests. The Monika madam she knew was effervescent and bubbly. It was only recently that the morose air had been embraced. How then, did she gel with the amma of this house? They were like chalk and cheese. Strange.

In the initial days, she used to drop in for a cup of tea and exchange pleasantries but the visits soon dwindled. At first, she thought that Sharada madam's curt nature had something to do with it. But it was only later that she came to know the real reason behind the distance. She was turning out to be a real muddle head. Speculating on situations that were not meant to be speculated upon. It was the upbringing she reasoned. Being concerned about each other was a way of life in their tiny village. But things were different with the city dwellers. Whatever it was, human beings were the same. They reacted in the exact same manner when faced with adversities. Societal status was hence not a barometer for emotional well-being. The rich and the poor faced the same struggles albeit, with slight modifications. Situations played out in a similar fashion; problems tackled along similar routes. The only difference lay in the strength of will. Mind mattered over design.

Mala believed that Gods plans could definitely be altered provided one made the right choice. Take her own case for instance. She should have considered suicide were she and her three children were to depend on her husband for a living. But she chose to live and support the drunkard as well. It was a moral duty she was obliged to shoulder. Same with Sharada madam as well she supposed. Although, in this instance, penury was not a word she would use. The family was doing quite well for themselves. And madam's word was the law. The family's coffers were under lock and key. Which was very well for the four of them. It was a strain for the madam but her husband provided her unfailing support and that was the key to the smooth functioning of this unit. The Pallikal members were on the right track.

Sanal vroomed about on an imaginary scooter and Mala moved with a deftness that narrowly avoided a collision. Her broom was tucked in; a reflex action on her part and the boy laughed in glee. The boy was the delight of this home. He was a happy child and pranced about like a deer, hopping on all fours sometimes. Once she had taken him along and he had bonded with her children in an instant. The four played a game of marbles until an errant one caught him on the cheek. Mala brought the boy home in fear, hoping against hope that her job would not be compromised. But Sanal's father deftly sidestepped a potential explosion by letting her leave immediately before the madam arrived on the scene. The next day was a strained affair with a tense Mala completing her duties in silence. As she prepared to leave, a packet was pressed into her hands. It was her dinner packet. Tears filled her eyes and she held on to Sharada madam's hands in gratitude.

"I'm very sorry for what happened yesterday madam. It was an accident. I know he is very dear to you. Please forgive me…"

"You do not have to apologize Mala. Children encounter such issues during playtime. Knowing me, you were smart enough to flee from the scene yesterday," gruff response followed the rueful grin.

"I would have bitten off your head," she continued and smiles were exchanged. "You know that he is dear to me considering my condition….." She broke away awkwardly. Clearing her throat, she resumed, "I am grateful to be living this life. It was never meant to come this far you know. I was a lost case. But I am hanging on… for the sake of my loved one's. They have given me a reason to hold on."

Mala looked on in wonder. This was her Sharada madam addressing her. They never shared personal details with each other. She was used to lamenting out her troubles to all who would care to listen. But madam here, she was different. She was so strong. Fearless. She was a fighter. Like Abbakka Chowta. Valiant even though death faced her.

Unaware of the strong feelings that were surging within Mala, Sharada continued, "I want Rashi to understand what she has been given. Understand the importance of her life. I am not a good speaker and my communication skills as far as she is concerned is unfortunately nonexistent but I hope that she will be brave and fight for her cause whatever be the situation. Her hatred for me will change one day and then, I know she will be my strongest ally." So, she knew. This mother knew that the girl burned with anger. Anger that was directed at the very individual that had given birth to her. Madam was a teacher no doubt and she knew the psyche of the ones under her care. But she was a seasoned fighter and would turn the situation to her advantage someday.

Mala left the house that evening in wonderment. She has been privy to a facet of character that had only been hinted upon, never revealed. Oh, the joy of being a woman. She fed her family with Sharada madam's offering with feelings that were akin to devotion. This was manna from the Gods. The pious woman had taught her something wholesome and valuable today

***

The fall and the stained dress satisfactorily concluded events for the day. Rashi preferred to lock herself up inside her room after the physical chastening. Her little transistor provided her solace during the down moments. Hindi melodies were sure-fire morale boosters. Her pep-up tonic during the morose times. She could lie in bed, look out the window and hum along all day long. Curl up and sleep too. And when the knock was sounded, she was obliged to join the rest of the members for the night meal. That could not be missed. The golden rule ensured that she would never have to go to bed on an empty stomach. That, was a relief considering the stubborn inner self that prodded and dared her to do just the opposite. Of course, she would never do that. Her mother's lovely curries and dishes were something to die for. Why carry the sulk right through the evening and ruin everyone's mood?

Her father would nonchalantly serve her double helpings and she would steal oblique looks at her stern-faced mother who had obviously noticed the furtive gesture but chose to remain silent. To her, the sympathy was one-sided. It made her meal-times enjoyable though. Sanal, the crowd pleaser would grin at her good naturedly and make short work of his plate's contents.

As for the schooltime, things went from bad to worse as expectations grew and her grades dipped in proportion. She began to wilt under the pressure. A neighbor's daughter Janani, good old Bhama, other cousins and children of the colleagues of her father seemed to be running a race to outperform each other. She, on the other hand, lagged far behind, made no friends, talked to no one and generally preferred her own company. Her OCD probably stems from this period and graced her routine when a career in physiotherapy was opted for. Obsessiveness about cleanliness, body hygiene, her looks, dressing, the books, shelves in their room, her closet, the way her clothes were folded, anything and everything that would take her far away from the rigor of formal studies took precedence.

Rashi did well, but not well enough. The goal that her mother fixed her sights on, was to be a distant dream; something that could never be attained. Over time, Rashi gave up on chasing the unachievable. That was not meant to be in any case. As long as a decent enough college offered her a seat without the hassle of being asked to pay anything extra apart from the annual fee, would be satisfactory was the shrewd guess. So, she would work towards that. Possibly that college in Mangalore? Anyplace but home would do well. She was sick of the place, her room, their home and most importantly, her mother. The toxic environment affected her to such an extent that she refused to watch over her brother or interact with him as he grew up. The only modicum of a relationship that remained with her father was retained and that was the farthest she was willing to go.

'Sometimes, I wonder about the harshness of the methods that my mother used to mete out. Wasn't I pretty enough? I knew I was on the watch. The ones that dared comment would rave about how fair I

Walk Away

was, how slim and well behaved. This used to incense my mother all the more and I began to withdraw into my shell the minute I watched the symptoms appear. Was it the fact that I was a normal child without any hint of the symptoms associated with a malaise? Perhaps she was jealous of her daughter since she did not have a normal childhood as I did. But I'm sure she would have been far happier than what I am now. Her mother treated her like a queen and here I was, the original misfit. A misfit in Sharada Ramakrishnan's world. They shouldn't have tried so hard for a child if this was how they were planning to bring it up.'

Rashi watched scores of parents pick and drop their children from school and their happy smiles and gaiety sucked the void further within her. She could not muster the energy required to smile back at Mala aunty nowadays. The lady used to watch her quite keenly, and offer a hesitant smile in sympathy. Sometimes her blood boiled at the pity-laced-glance and she would avoid looking in her direction the next time.

It was on one such evening that the woman dropped by her room to sweep, mop and finally, clean the washroom. As she disappeared inside, the sounds of scrubbing and swishing of water was heard followed by the flushing of the toilet bowl. Mala reappeared only to resume sweeping of the room. Rashi lifted her feet from the floor and sat cross legged on the bed, engrossed in a book. After a while, she realized that the rhythmic sounds had ceased and curiosity beckoned. A pair of kohl rimmed eyes that contained puzzlement, met her gaze. Mala aunty was wondering about her, she reckoned. She lifted her eyebrows casually and the lady hastily dropped her eyes.

"Always studying aren't you little madam. Such a nice daughter madam has. You will grow big and make her proud, just like her plan."

The last sentence incensed me. What was this 'her plan?' Didn't my father have a say in all this?

Mala aunty noted the change in expression and became alarmed. Trying to cover up for the error she had committed, she added in haste, "You are part of such a wonderful family. A loving father. A mother that cares. See how she cooks non-vegetarian food for you in spite of being a vegetarian. That's sacrifice. You will understand when you grow up dear."

Oh, I understood all the sacrifices very well. And what about the ones I make, day in and out? Can a bleeding lip or bruised skin make up for lost time? Would she indulge in such behavior with her children with unfailing regularity?

Mala was now at a loss for words. The girl was correct to a fault. The mismatch between mother and daughter was glaringly evident. The chasm was too wide to be repaired. She did not know how best to explain. Illiterate and uncouth she was. But she would make one last attempt. A final desperate try in the hope that the child would relent, reconsider.

Taking a deep breath, she explained, "In our village, it is said that a mother is the force that brings a jewel to life. Just as my children are precious to me, so are you to your mother. I have an additional burden to carry on my shoulders until I die and the same goes with your mother. But as far as your amma is concerned, I know that her focus is only trained on her daughter - you. Have you noticed how she pampers your brother and lets him be but she is the very opposite of that with you? That only means one thing; you need to earn her respect. Give her what she wants and see her change before your very eyes. Try this and see the results. You will find that all this time has been wasted for something so trivial. I am an uneducated simpleton little madam but I have some experience as a mother. Hopefully your anger will vanish and you will understand your mother a little better. The happiness of this home depends only upon you."

Rashi listened to the monologue dumbly, her rage mounting by the second. Dressing her down, was she? This incompetent woman? How dare she assess the situation as though it was her life to begin with and pronounce judgement? Rashi uttered a cry of rage and stomped out of the room.

Mala's shoulders slumped in defeat. Perhaps this mother and daughter combination had some unknown karma working against them. Only time could heal their souls. She picked up the mop in her hands, rinsed it and began to swab the floor.

***

                                                    Walk Away

Rashi walked outside and around her home in incoherent rage. She was furious about the house-help empathizing with her mother, her employer. Has she not watched the struggles and torment she was facing? Day in and out, she suffered humiliation and preferential treatment at the hands of her mother. Her father would always remain mum, indirectly offering support to his wife. Her brother well, his grin sometimes made her want to knock it off his face. Scatter a few of those teeth onto the ground as well, she muttered to herself in anger.

When would all this end? She would be entering her teens pretty soon, so any form of escape was not to be expected in the near future. She hated this home as well as her parents and sibling. All she wanted was her grandmother to reappear and gather her in her arms. She would sob her heart out, she knew. She also knew that she would be embraced and kissed. Her tears would be wiped away with a smile and her favorite sweetmeat fed to her, one bite at a time, ever so lovingly.

Rashi felt all the hurt and the anger within her melt away. One kind word, a sweet gesture, one smile; was all that she needed. She would give it her all and start anew. But that was never to be. She was a lost cause. Not good enough for anything.

But wait…. one thing that Mala aunty mentioned, made sense. Not the one where she asked her to cower and beg. But the one that hinted at a possible escape for her from this hellhole. "Plan a career and work your way towards that. Your freedom lies in that direction Rashi," her mind directed her.

So, what was she to do? Start working from school?

"No, silly. Draw up a list. Add your likes and dislikes to it. Strike off the ones you feel are unfit. Slowly the picture will seem clearer to you."

"Give me an example," she asked the inner voice.

"Write down the popular career choices usually taken up by everyone. Medicine for example, or engineering, architecture, marketing, even a central govt. job like father. Not to mention, inclusion of that all-important tag; homemaker to the list as well!" the voice ended on a deprecatory note.

"Hmm. Interesting. With the exception of the medical field, I don't think anything interests me as much. I should probably give sciences a go, don't you think?"

"Yep. There you go. Now narrow down further to the fields of your choice, something within this sphere and by the time you complete your schooling, you are good to go. Don't think that a doctor's coat would suit you though."

"And why ever not? I would look cool."

"You would, yes. But your temperament won't."

"Hello. Now who is deciding my fate here? What else do think I would be good at, pray?"

Alter ego replied without hesitation, "A place where you will feel safe, away from all the prying eyes, busy in your own little world, happy with your hectic schedule and basking in the respect of your patients and colleagues. That's how I see you content and happy."

A.E's confident reply stunned Rashi. She was absolutely correct. Rashi wanted a hidey hole where she could curl up and feel safe. She needed to feel important and respected for the work she did. And yes, she needed to fend for herself. Lots and lots of it. She was done with wearing all the hand me downs and having to look perpetually grateful. Her choices would range from the expensive to the smart and chic. Not for once would she drape inferior products on her body. All this and more, with the money she earned. She would work her way up, accept double shifts and live off her savings like a queen. That was what she wished for. And now that the matter had been resolved, Rashi's mood lightened considerably. She felt the jaunt reappear within her as she walked into the house, refreshed at heart. Mala watched the girl come in and felt her heart skip. She sensed the sudden transformation. And as she watched Rashi walk past her, a grateful smile was flashed at her.

***

"That's a sickly child." Hmm.

"Fragile as well." Sickly. Fragile.

These were words she had listened to often enough while growing

                                          Walk Away

up. The constant litany had torn into her. She knew that she was physically weak. The mental challenges associated with these; all the unseen hurdles, had to be crossed.

When Sharada was born, the family was overjoyed. A girl child was a gift to be treasured. Fair with limpid eyes, the infant cooed sweetly at the visitors. But very soon, the dark clouds begun to converge. Listlessness, constant crying, delayed milestones, and a marked reluctance towards any activity that would lead to a depletion in energy were noticed. When concerned relatives suggested a visit to a specialist and the result was proclaimed, the emotional upheaval was acute. The happiness that began to decrease from the time the verdict was pronounced, abandoned the family as it was placed under the scanner. The observations increased to such an extent that; the mother began to shun her regular duties. Very soon, a cook and a domestic helper were assigned to carry out all the regular tasks within the household.

Narayanan and Latha decided to focus all of their energies on Sharada, their precious bundle of joy and cocoon it within their love. An invisible safety net was thus designed and formed over the course of the years that allowed for the child to grow and improve as an individual. Latha began work as an Anganwadi* teacher and Narayanan took up an admin job in a private concern. The child attended regular school.

Having briefed all the teachers and classmates of successive classes, Sharada was not subjected to the rigors of academics. And that helped her sail through school. A helper was appointed to pick and drop her from the school compound. She was not allowed to carry her bags. Mohan uncle did that for her. She was not allowed to ride a bicycle. Once she pleaded her cause and promptly turned pale and wan. Poor Mohan uncle disappeared from the scene as well. Since then, Sharada stopped requesting people to aid her for things that seemed normal to them but was not, in her case. It meant that she would have to forego their comfortable presence. A sacrifice once made was sacrifice enough.

Thus grew Sharada; placid, undemanding and unaccustomed to the rigors of life. Visits to the doctor revealed that her constitution was sensitive thereby resulting in her vegetarian diet. Unsurprisingly enough, her parents also switched to the same. What their Sharada would have to forego, they would too. Sharada was thus smothered in a sea of affection and knew no want. There was no respite from the cushion she was cradled in.

But the girl wanted something different. She wanted to play, swim, run like the wind, laugh like one possessed. Indulge in physical games with her cousins, ride a bicycle, climb trees. What she had seen was what she wished to experience. But the disappearance of Mohan uncle changed all of that. She understood the rules of the game. 'Sickly' was a word she despised. She was not 'fragile' either. The moniker had however stuck.

Her friends avoided her and so did her cousins. They shared secrets that she was not privy to. To them, she seemed to be the sneaky kind. And that hurt. For she was neither. She was quiet, withdrawn and would never misplace the trust placed on her. Wild stories shared of exploits by common friends made the rounds of which none would reach poor Sharada. And the distancing slowly turned her into a recluse. She turned sullen and seldom smiled. The doctors described this as 'a phase.' She was flitting though the normal urges one had as a teenager. That would soon subside.

"And what of her health?"

"Oh, that was stable enough. One could not predict the outcome. But if they (the parents) had been successful in holding it all together, who knew, further miracles could be expected."

Emboldened and hugely elated, the parents offered a minor leeway, away from the rigid lifestyle guidelines that should be followed. Sharda could now sit and watch her cousins play. She could accompany them to places that offered entertainment and was not too far away from their house or the doctor's clinic. Sharada began to smile and speak out a bit.

On one occasion, when she watched her cousins play, she gathered the injured Gowri and helped her inside. Dabbing a cold compress at her lips, it was cousin Ramakrishnan that sat alongside the sobbing girl with a concerned air. When he passed the ice-cube encased kerchief to her and their fingers touched, she felt a mild jolt. Their gazes met although he thought nothing of it. From that moment on, Sharada watched him

                                    Walk Away

like a hawk.

Here was a being with a heart that was soft as cotton and a smile to die for. The relationship would be consanguineous she knew, having read of it in books but she cared two hoots for custom. She needed a weapon to arm herself with and Cousin Ramakrishnan would be ideal. Although he did not have an inkling of the events that would lead to their union, Sharada felt that fate had lent her two sets of hands and an extra compartment in her brain to compensate for her physical deficit. She would toil hard, get a degree and, make sure that her mother's job came her way. That, along with the pension her parents would receive would ensure her future well-being. Marriage was only the next step in the turn of events.

Of course, her husband would fall in line with what she did. In the end, they all went along with the scheming, unaware of the lure that had been carefully planned in advance. The ones that accompanied Sharada on her path to life gave up being the persons they were simply because she was impaired and they did not want to turn into spokes that upset the balance of the wheel.

Placid Sharada thus turned into her shrewder version, one that no one could fathom, such was the cunning with which she cloaked herself. She observed more, planned more and spoke minimally. It was when she was thwarted that her true self loomed. It was as if mother earth herself would quake before her fury. In no time though, the opposition would meekly cower. It was not fear that led to the acquiescing but love - the emotion that bound everyone to Sharada. The fear of suddenly losing this soul. The fear of an impending grief that would devastate the family. Narayanan uncle and Latha aunty would be bereft of a child. Their life had never been their own. Such was the fierce love they had for her. Their only child.

And so, everyone kept mum when she lashed out. And over the course of time, learnt to accept it as fate. Acceptance, in the name of family. A life for peace. A life for harmony. A life in exchange for a lifetime of happiness. Until it lasted that is.

What was not accounted for, was the mind that was trained during the time the body was being cossetted. A mind that was sharp, scored like steel, one that sniffed out all possibilities, spared no one were the impact to strike her or her offspring and most of all, a willpower that was unbending, unyielding and hard as rock.

How else do you think that a girl who could hardly take a few steps without the labored breathing, walk the extra mile, produce a set of progenies that delighted everyone including her and create an efficient household until she succumbed at the age of sixty-five, to the very malaise that has been destined to snuff out her soul in her early years? This then, was Sharada Ramakrishnan. The original fighter. The one who defied all odds. And the one who was determined to make her child Rashi even stronger. All this mollycoddling would weaken her and for what she would face in future, she needed to be Sharada twice over to confront and walk away with her spine erect. It was her intuition that guided her from the very beginning. The girl would not have her to lean on when it mattered and should that turn into an impediment, her spirit would support and guide her along. Sharada would retain her wings if her feet were cut off. She would cloak her child from the test of time and deposit her gently into a place where she would find herself and regrow.

***

Esther remembered her early life; the friends, visits to the church (they were Mangalorean Catholics), familiar cooking smells and, being pranked by her elder brothers. Seafood was abundant since they hailed from a coastal region along with rice and coconut being a staple part of their daily meals. Esther and her three siblings attended the St.Anne Catholic Higher Secondary School. The route they took to school remained unchanged right from the time they were enrolled to the time they passed out. Esther's passion lay in the sciences and she chose to work her way through college after completion of high school. Opting for a Bachelor's degree in Physics, she graduated from the Subaiyya College of Arts and Sciences and was now eager to try her hand in an environment where her knowledge could put to use. A short stint at her alma mater as senior teacher of Physics left her feeling unsatisfied.

She craved for excitement and hoped to climb up the rung of success. Teaching students and returning to the room she had occupied since the time she was born, depressed her.

Accordingly, a trip to Mumbai - the land of dreams was planned. She had heard that it was a place one could live the fast life in comfort and that suited her current disposition. The farewell she received was tearful. A huge horde of friends and relatives dropped in to bid her goodbye. Theirs was a well-known family. So, her decision pretty much reached the ears of all and sundry. Her parents and brothers were against the idea. Their girl had turned into a rebel. It surprised them. Haji chacha, their fishmonger airily dismissed the idea as being frivolous. The girl would take a trip and return. She would calm down once she realized how difficult things could turn out to be when you had to fend for yourself. The argument at home was ongoing, the questions directed at her were several - Where was she planning to stay? Where would she work? How would she earn and how would that suffice? How would she cook and look after herself in a world that had no time for anyone or anything?

Esther however, remained firm having anticipated these concerns and stuck to her decision. She had already reached out to a former schoolmate who promised to help her out. Philipa was a true blue Mumbaiite who knew every nook and corner of the city. She assured her that securing a job was not an issue and neither was staying as a PG. There were enough number of homes that let out spaces within their homes at affordable rates that would provide adequate security as far as a newcomer was concerned.

And that was how she boarded the second-class sleeper of the Mangalore-Mumbai express, settling herself for the long journey in the upper berth, reading and dreaming of a wonderful life she would soon lead. A fast car, bungalow, a handsome husband, a bunch of kids frolicking around the house and pots of money to spend on. The thought cheered her tremendously and as the train chugged on, Esther dozed in happiness.

Apart from the intermittent visit to a smelly toilet at the end of the compartment, she immersed herself in songs that played on her

Walkman. The familiarity of the songs lulled her into a feeling of being within her room, back home. Often times, a particular odor from down below presumably, the family sharing home cooked food would assail her senses. For although Esther had been provided packed meals for the duration of her journey, she still felt a pang of nostalgia for the world she was leaving behind. It was her mother and the food she cooked that she would miss the most. Her elder brother was married and the second was carrying on with his girlfriend. The third was pursuing a higher degree at the college of Technology in Udupi. Esther's boyfriend, a member of their church was in Canada at present and they planned on getting married after a year or two. Ideally, she wanted him to come down and settle in Mumbai and live the life she wanted. But he asked her to be patient. She had to gain enough work experience before they took the next step. That would be the decider in getting to where they planned to be.

Although she had no idea how life would treat her, her naivete provided for the confidence she needed to think of her future in a positive way. Melvin laughed at her innocence. This was like writing down things in water. The overlapping ripples would swallow the words carved out that instant. There should be a constant for the words to be effective. Esther in all the freshness of her youth imagined that life would offer her roses and Melvin did not want to disappoint her. He hoped that he would be able to give her a life that she craved for and soon. It would be a bad idea if she insisted on settling in the city of Mumbai. He did not intend to fly down and live amongst the grime and chaos. An idyllic life in Montreal suited his mindset. But no matter, he would convince her to drop everything and fly into his arms. He couldn't wait for too long. Two years seemed an awfully long time to be apart.

***

Mumbai. The land of hope. Presided by Mumbadevi - patron goddess and benefactor of the Koli community, the original settlers of the famed city. Seven islands that were banded together to turn into India's formidable trading center and now home to an amazing assortment of people from all walks of life.

Monika Esther D'Silva alighted from the train and looked around her in awe. Philipa had called. She would reach the station in ten minutes. Mumbai traffic and the chaos accompanying it, was legendary. Philipa was getting close. Her autorickshaw was inching along and when she called, Esther could hear the honks of cars and a multitude of voices in the background. The din around her was deafening as well. Never had she come across such a crowd, thicketed together and pressing forward like packed sardines within a tin can.

Esther placed her suitcase on the ground with a sigh. Her arms hurt. She had packed the entire contents of her wardrobe into her suitcase and a travel bag. Her precious makeup kit and a few books added to the weight. She had her trusty phone in hand and a few thousand rupees in the bank. What more did she require for the moment except for a roof above her head, good food to eat and some sight-seeing along the chowks and by-lanes of the city? She knew that Mumbai's street food and pavement shops were the most fun things to explore. Philipa promised her a run-in along the famed Juhu beach as well as visits to the local churches. They would ransack the cheap eateries and pick magazines and books from the random second-hand shops, visit theatres to watch the A-list actors in action and hoot and crow at the riotous scenes. She was holed up in a room let out by an old aunt from Goa who was basically a cool cat. Apart from the timings that they were supposed to adhere to, Aunty Sandra was okay with anything that they did.

She was all alone, explained Philipa and her children were settled in the UK and Portugal. Her Anglo-Indian ancestry allowed them a favorable entry into the country of their choice and they had not made any mention of coming by to visit her so far. Poor Aunty Sandra. Her loss was Philipa and Esther's gain basically. She was jolly and easy going and had her favorite tipple in the evening, a peg of gin and lime cordial. So, if they were to make her happiness last longer, simply gift her a bottle of her favorite and you were good to go.

Esther listened to her friend's chat non-stop while she absorbed the busy throng speeding past in all directions. On one occasion, she caught the auto driver unashamedly listening to their conversation. When she dug her elbow into Philipa, her friend chided the driver in Marathi. He replied to her with a laugh but continued to watch them through the vehicle's rearview mirror.

"Pips, I need a job dear… and quickly," interjected Esther worriedly.

"That is not an issue Madam. Mumbadevi welcomes all here," assured the driver quickly.

The two friends looked at each other.

Philipa squeezed Esther's arm and said, "Trust me hon and don't worry. I have arranged a temp job for you in my office. That way, we will travel together. It will be fun. And you will get to use your makeup kit regularly and hunt for a wealthy bloke at the same time."

Esther flushed in embarrassment and stole a quick glance at the driver. He averted his eyes this time. Philipa needed to guard her chatty tongue. Sometimes she was overtly brash.

"Bhaiyya*, go around the circle and under the bridge to the right. The fourth house up ahead, the one with the green painted gate, that old house…" she pointed in the direction of the bungalow and continued, "yes, that's it, please stop here." As they hopped out, she paid the driver and bid him goodbye. Apparently, he wanted a bit more than the fare and when Pips got ready to argue back, Esther dug into her purse and paid him an extra hundred. She did not want to begin her new life on a note of displeasure. She was getting to live her dream and the route had to be planned just right. Philipa glared at her in displeasure but the grinning driver offered them a mock half-salute and sped away.

Aunty Sandra heard the commotion by the gate and was waiting by the door. She peered at the newcomer through her half-moon spectacles and smiled in delight. She had baked a cake to help Esther feel at home and indicated that they could tuck in almost immediately. The hungry girls exchanged a round of pleasantries and washed their hands by the tableside. They were served warm slices of the cake along with a pot of black tea. Lunch was ready if they felt like it but the girls politely declined. Philipa needed to sort through her clothes and get them washed and ironed for the upcoming week. Esther needed to rest awhile too. They could talk later.

Aunty Sandra agreed to all this with reluctance. She was looking forward to a day of laughter and small talk. Never mind, she had the TV to pass time. They could slip into a comfortable routine once Esther was settled and felt better.

Life turned out to be pleasant and gay. Since Esther has been brought up in a restrictive household, life in Mumbai turned out to be the best gamble she had ever made. The first week was spent exploring all the quaint little by-lanes in and around the area she was living in. Borivilli she felt, had an old-world charm to it but reflected the casual sheen of modern living. Once the hustle and bustle of the office goers gradually waned and settled down, she would spend time chit-chatting with Aunty Sandra over breakfast and coffee.

Getting to know the bungalow she lived in was the next task. The house was at least a hundred years old. From its green painted wooden arches that decorated the door lintels, to the patterned tiled floors, the intricately carved mantelpiece, an ornate fountain that had long dried up, iron taps that creaked and groaned before the water gushed out, the ancient well by the side of the house that still served up sweet sparkling water, an ancient electric cooking range that was presumably imported from Great Britain and worked quite well considering Aunty Sandra did all of her cooking on it as of old, the four-poster bed with cotton mattresses that came with a detachable mosquito net, an attic that brimmed with brass colanders, picture frames and myriad relics from the past, and a tiny cellar that was now used to stock seasonings and preserves as well as salted fish and pork. Esther marveled at the energy of the sprightly eighty-year-old landlady who remained a bundle of cheeriness and positivity.

She had developed a soft corner for the lady and therefore took care to avoid conversations about her family for the latter seemed to turn morose at times. Aunty Sandra's children and grandchildren never visited her in the recent past ensconced as they were, in the world they once struggled to emigrate to. Esther worried about the times aunty would fall sick. She had no medical insurance and no credit cards in hand. Her bimonthly trips to the post office and banks ensured that her pension and rent covered all her needs. But what if she fell ill or something worse happened, she argued with Philipa in all fierceness? They were Aunty Sandra's companions no doubt and could take care of her to the best of their ability but it was the duty of the family to look in at times as well, wasn't it? Didn't the kind heart provide for them when they were young? She had been their emotional cushion and moral support during the times the family numbers burgeoned. The least they could do was to take her with them.

"You are getting attached to aunty, Esther. She's a feisty one. Do you think she would give up her independence and hare off to a country she's only heard about and not accustomed to? No way hon. She's a hardcore Mumbaiite. Her plans are to die in this house surrounded by the things she loves and be buried by her husband's side."

"But she's old and frail. We are her only support. What if something happens when I start work from say, next week?"

"Don't work yourself up for nothing darl. We'll tackle anything that comes up 'if' and 'when' it happens. For now, let us all live our lives and be happy. She's full of life and that's how we want her to be right?"

And Esther had to reluctantly end the conversation at the time.

M/s Samatva Financials Ltd was a fairly burgeoning enterprise that had its beginnings in a small two-roomed flat in Bandra. About a decade later, it expanded its reach into the world of finance via. the share markets as well as the automobile industry and was now exploring the niche retail market of priority goods as well. The office was a hive of activity when Esther entered the spacious, brightly lit interior accompanied by Philipa. Her friend hurried inside after ensuring that she would be called by a member of the HR team for a brief chat.

"A receptionist?" she squealed in disbelief as Philipa outlined her grand strategy. She could work her way up was the assurance. Her diction was fairly good and she understood Hindi very well. She could pick up the local slang quickly this way and some workable Marathi as well and that would help her man the front office. Getting into the admin side would be easier after two or three years. For a beginner with no experience in office work, this was a Godsent and moreover, she, Philipa was around to keep an eye on her.

Esther nervously faced the interviewer across the table. She was perched on the edge of her seat. Her face belied the butterflies fluttering somewhere around the region of her stomach and her poor heart. The interviewer glanced at her papers.

"Teacher?"

Nod.

"Physics?"

Double nod.

"How does that bring you here?" The man hmm'ed and haw'ed for a while and picked up the phone.

"Give me extension twenty-five," was the terse command.

Presumably, Philipa was going to be quizzed.

"Lady, you have got me a teacher. What am I going to do with this candidate? I don't think that her qualification fits the profile we are looking for."

Animated conversation flowed from the other side as the man's eyebrows rose and he glowered in indecision. With a deep sigh, he said, "Well, if you say so. Let us give it thirty days. I do not have time to spare beyond that. You know that Neha leaves in a month, right?"

After a curt exchange of words, she was asked to join duty the following day. The task was to orient herself with everything that the outgoing employee had been handling. This included filing, following up on calls, send and receive mails and faxes, post reminders, oversee the decoration and caterers in the event of an office party, ensure that the pantry stocks were always replenished, handle the petty cash counter and of course, the mandatory phone calls that had to be received and passed which was in fact, her primary job.

Esther walked out of the room in a haze as her head whirled. How on earth was she to handle the entire gamut of duties singlehandedly? This Neha seemed to be a superwoman. Philipa rushed out and gave her a tight hug. She was glibly reassured that she would be as superefficient as her predecessor. Neha gently smiled at her and offered a hand in congratulation. Esther spent the next hour in an rickshaw, enjoying the ride and making the call to her family and Aunty Sandra. She wanted the old lady to hear the good news before she even reached home. Stopping to buy a Vada Pav - the lady's favorite, and two chole samosa chaat for the two of them, Esther finally smiled.

She had done it. Secured a job for herself. With Philipa's help of course. Her first step towards achieving independence and financial security was within her reach. Mumbadevi - she was on her way to achieving her dream. Esther tapped her way through unfamiliar territory. Philipa's spare phone had been given to her and her precious Nokia was now relegated to a junk filled drawer. After successfully messaging Melvin, an attempt was made to click a selfie within the confines of the moving vehicle. There. A decent head shot minus the smile was examined. Not cheery enough but she refrained from trying out another. So, the image was captioned and sent all the way to Mangalore, where her family awaited the good news.

***

Mala watched madam Monika out of the corner of her eyes. She seemed happier today. Perhaps she understood the lady better than most and that included Pritam sir. She has seen her madam blossom into a woman, happy within the comfort of her home, content with what she has. She reveled in the love and care provided by her husband and together, they had built themselves a safe haven away from eyes that pried. It was a different facet they had evolved from and one she has been witness to. Five years was a long time and much water has flown under the bridge. Monika madam's silhouette has toned and she seems more youthful today. The chirpiness has disappeared though. She had once possessed a kind of cheer, a gaiety that was infectious. This drew admiring glances her way. Mala on the other hand, was pregnant with her second child although she was way younger than madam.

Ensconced in a small *kholi** young Mala led a life of penury. The girl-turned-woman was also forced to endure the torturous and routine groping of an inebriated husband. And yes, he was addicted to his first love from the time she could remember. Their room was an unplastered square space that consisted of a rough cement floor with a curtained corner serving as the kitchen. The bathing and *sandaas** area was separate but common for all. Mala found it shameful to rush into the toilet after pandering to her husband's nightly demands. There were

Walk Away

eyes that watched and smirked, for the shanty was an assorted cluster of fabricated walls and roofs that did not offer much by way of privacy. Every sneeze, grunt and whispered conversation carried through with the result that everyone knew each other's story quite well. So, when Mala rushed to wash herself every night, her neighbors would laugh in amusement.

Come daytime and her shyness would evaporate as the kholi would empty itself of its occupants. There was no one she confided to even otherwise. This was Mumbai city she was living in. Here, everyone worked - man or woman. The shanty was steeped in filth since open drains and rotting garbage dotted the perimeter. Narrow paths snaked through its center and offshoots that offered connectivity were as narrow as the width of a child's slim shoulder. It was no wonder that the community that lived there was a close knit one considering the proximity.

Mala's first child was born in the comfort of her village and she returned after three months with the infant. The nightly pattern continued unabated but luckily Mala conceived only after Madan, her first born turned two. Prasad had by then turned erratic in his behavior and often stayed away from work. Money was scarce and she turned desperate. Her *mangalsutra* had been sold and so was the nose pin. One look at her husband sleeping throughout the day, head lolling, legs splayed wide was enough to make her puke.

Gathering Madan, she walked out of her kholi one fine day. The one place she knew, seemed to be closing in. The hunger pang was so acute, that her concern for the new one growing within her belly grew. Madan sniffled in distress but tagged along obediently. Mala blindly walked down the route that offered her freedom. One part of her held back, urging caution while the other prodded her to continue. The duo walked on ahead and reached the highway and continued along its side. She remembered the steady sun beating down on them and her mouth seemed parched. How she came upon the green gates and called out for a glass of water was something she had no recollection of but the kindness offered by Aunty Sandra revived her instantly.

Aunty Sandra had taken pity on her and offered her a job. And while she worked, her son was looked after by the old lady. He was taught the English letters and all the queer songs associated with the language. It had been a relief. The work kept her occupied besides giving her the much-needed financial support. The two room-mates Philipa and Esther contributed their share to help ease out her troubles. They were a happy twosome and her heart was glad for she had missed out on the laughter. Madan too, was getting along with everyone though inclined to naughtiness.

Mala remembered being enamored of the stately home. The rooms lent an aura of an era that had passed. An old gramophone sometimes blared out haunting melodies and Aunty Sandra hummed along as she paced from room to room. Madan gave her company as he hung on to the hem of her dress. Madan was Aunty Sandra's constant companion as she was his playmate. Old and the young cooed, gurgled, lisped and laughed together and time simply flew by.

Philipa and Esther were best friends. They worked in the same company, different divisions, she was made to understand. They ate together, shopped together, went to work together and came back together. Their lives melded together seamlessly and the five bonded together as a unit. Esther was the prettier of the two opined Mala although Philipa was gregarious and had her fair share of admirers. Esther's boyfriend she was made to understand would come looking for her soon and all her freewheeling options would disappear on his arrival. Mala envied at how the two had their lives neatly plotted and played out to perfection. Her child was growing and her belly was distending. Three months to go and she would have to contend with another mouth to feed.

Philipa and Esther were excited about something. A new boyfriend was on the cards and Esther seemed genuinely happy for her friend. Now the two couldn't wait to get hitched. When would the lucky day come, wondered the two. Philipa walked about with a distracted air and Esther would say something funny at which the two would erupt in a fit of giggles. Mala would smile and observe them. Life seemed so uncomplicated for the two friends.

A month passed by and a minor disaster struck in the form of a fall. Aunty Sandra asked for a chair to be pushed towards her as she readied herself for a cup of tea. She stood facing the giant dining table and waited

Walk Away

for little Madan to push the chair towards her to sit on. But the child misjudged the distance and when Aunty Sandra fell, the muffled thud rocked the quietness of the home. Mala discovered the old lady writhing on the floor in pain and the boy crying beside her. She immediately dialed Philipa's number and asked them to rush home. When the two friends arrived, they were accompanied by a young bearded man. He seemed concerned and helped them carry their aged companion to her room. Old Doctor Irani, their kindly neighbor, who was also the same age as aunty Sandra as well as her old friend, came by and gave her a thorough physical examination.

While there were no breaks or sprain, what was worrisome was the acute pain suffered at the base of her spine. A possible coccyx (tail bone) fracture was the grave pronouncement. There was no cure for the condition. Bed rest for a month or more depending on the severity would help in alleviating the condition. And, Sandra's next of kin would have to be informed. Her children needed to be called.

The group turned silent at this. They would have to ask the lady to part with the information. She was notoriously reticent about details related to her family. Doctor Irani nodded in understanding and was seen off by Philipa. Mala watched aunty Sandra in concern. Esther stood by her bedside and held her hand. Madan stood by her side, his face glum. The newcomer stood watching the trio from the opposite side of the room. What caught Mala's attention was the way he looked at madam Esther. There was a shine in his eyes that was quickly masked the minute Philipa came by. This intrigued her considering the fact that the young man was known as the latter's boyfriend. The one who was supposedly planning to propose a lifetime of love. Has she been mistaken or was she imagining things? She has been married long enough to know the difference between love and lust. Fate had subjected her to a combination of the two for years but for a moment, right that instant, she felt that she was not mistaken.

A loud groan startled the assembled group and they instantly converged around the ailing old woman.

Mala hurried into the kitchen to warm some water for Aunty Sandra and prepare coffee for their guest.

"Thank you for being with us today Preet," said Philipa gratefully and he smiled in return.

Esther was overwhelmed with emotion. Poor aunty Sandra. She was in so much pain. She gulped in anxiety and hugged Madan as they kept a strict vigil by her bedside. It was turning dark outside and Mala switched on the overhead lights as well as the lights within the compound. She offered a cup of coffee to their kind-hearted guest who seemed to have a crush on Esther and not Philipa. The coffee exchanged hands and was sipped on in silence. After a while, aunty Sandra drifted off to sleep and the guest stood up to leave. Esther hardly noticed and neither did the child stir, such was their vigil. Philipa escorted her man to the door and there they stood speaking softly for a few minutes. After a while, he gently touched her on the shoulder and left. Funny, that did not seem to be the kind of romance Philipa was expecting, thought Mala. Her hunch seemed to be growing stronger by the minute. She would however, guard her tongue and watch the play of events as it panned out.

Back in the room, Philipa motioned for Esther to follow her. "You have been given a two-week paid leave. Preet asked me to tell you. Isn't he a great guy? Said he would drop by once in a while to see how aunty Sandra's doing."

Esther looked at her uncomprehendingly as Philipa went on, "I cannot afford to stay on and look after aunty. But since both you and Mala will be around, I feel better already."

"But… but, who will man the front office?" spluttered Esther in a daze.

"He asked us to not worry about that. The company will function like it has always done. Aah the guy…gosh. Those dreamy eyes….," gushed Philipa as she hugged herself tightly.

The poor girl was all over the man while he had his eyes fixed firmly on her friend. The friend however, was unaware of the new development. Wah. Wah.

Mala snorted in amusement and the two women looked at her enquiringly. Shrugging her shoulders, she went in to call Madan and feed him dinner.

***

Sahaj was turning desperate. His advances were not being considered. The tough guy in him turned meek and gooey but that did not help either. He hoped for a smile, a look, a kind word… anything that would come his way and offer him a good night's rest. But that was not meant to be. His paramour - the love of his life, had a heart of stone.

He knew he was being ridiculed. The droopy eyed caricature that walked around, feet dragging, heart wedged within the palm of his hands; well, that was him. Sad songs - the ones where the hero loses his love to a tragic event and designed to bring out the sniffles, were played by his friends who loitered about on the streets and would not hesitate to pass up on a moment to needle him. He pretended not to notice. Rejection hung over him like a cloud and as for his loafer-cum-destitute friends, who had not an ounce of remorse for his condition, he cared the least. The object of his affection had a tight grip on him and the wastrels could do what they wanted. It was their lives to fritter away. For him though, there was on the horizon, a shimmer. An optimism within him pushed at him, strengthened his resolve to make a last-ditch effort to change her mind.

"Mamay* you are not her type. Why do you even think of it?"

Sahaj's friend Nitin was blunt. He meant well but this time, his plain-speak was not welcome.

"Orey* just shut it. This is not a dating game. I am all out to get married. And the lady is not just a crush. She's my world… my first love."

"Keep dreaming Saho. she'll kick your butt and walk over you. Mark my words. They are high-class folks. They look down on us, you, me and the idiots over there," Nitin indicated the motley gang lounging under a tree.

The warning was conveyed in a gruff tone. It pre-empted a feeling of unease in Sahaj's heart. One look at his glum face and Nitin's heart melted. Giving his friend a half-hug, he bade him sit on the bench in front of a tea stall and ordered two cups of sulaimani and buns.

"Mamay, you are in love. Enjoy the feeling while it lasts. For people like us, whose daily earnings keep our families intact, there is not the slightest chance of an angel like her coming into our lives. All I can tell you is, anticipate the results and be prepared. Else you will fall down like a pack of cards and scatter away when the winds blow. There will only be your good old friend; this Nitin sitting beside you, and your poor mother to console you in your grief."

"What if she says yes?" warring mind tussled against the hope that arose.

Nitin sighed wearily. "Then all good Saho. But think of the future as well. Will she stay in your one-roomed flat? Will she adjust with your mother? What about living expenses? And her parents? Do you think that they will accept you or the situation? Be practical Mamay. All these things happen in the movies. Violins playing in the background, rose petals in the air, the two of you dancing around trees etc. Unfortunately…" the words trailed away and his sideways glance spoke volumes. The deliberate look was as showy as the films he had just been criticizing.

"Man, you are one pessimistic lout. Having a family has turned you into a big bore. Frankly, your sermonizing has increased my resolve. I am going to try my luck with her tomorrow."

Nitin gave a short bark of laughter at this. "So be it man. But don't tell me that you were not warned. When you fall flat on your face, just get up and don't look at anyone. Catch the next bus out to nowhere. Frankly, I should have thought better than to advise you. Wasted fifteen minutes of my time for nothing."

Glares were exchanged. Finally, Nitin sped away on his bike. Sahaj turned morose after his departure. The anger felt good. It was a welcome change from the dullness he was experiencing these days. She was like a drug that had entered his system. One, that refused to let go and couldn't do without as well. He wondered if he was a fool. Were all the fools that were afflicted with the syndrome think and behave like him? He had led a pretty straightforward life until the time he had set sights on her. She was the original golden goddess. Ethereal and pure.

That she was committed to her job was clear. And he was proud of the fact. She might not need him but he did. He wanted her in his life. Forever. That would give him the zeal to bring down the heavens into her world. He would move the earth and moon and cosset her in luxury.

                                                    Walk Away

Everything that money could buy, would be hers. She would not regret her decision even for a day.

Sahaj was a man of his word. His friends would swear on that. His darling would understand that tomorrow. He would tell her so.

Half an hour had flown by and Sahaj was still working it out. A stray dog has cannily snuck away with the half-eaten bun he had in his hand but the lovelorn youth hardly noticed. A sudden gust of wind broke his chain of thoughts and he shivered. Tomorrow morning would be too late. It had to be now or never. He would wait by the gates of the hospital and speak to her.

A rose was what he needed. A red rose. That, and a diary milk bar. The sure-fire formula worked well in movies. She would be pleased and he was sure of that. Sahaj hurried to buy the two important things. This was his valentine moment and he would not screw it up.

***

Monika opened the door to let Mala in. Mala was accompanied by her firstborn Madan as well as her three-year-old girl - Bulbul and little Sheru*. Apologizing profusely, she bade her children sit on the floor near the wall of the living room. They were not allowed to run amok and disturb the serene setting. Monika was however, delighted with the appearance of the unexpected guests. Her day brightened considerably. Walking up to Madan, she hugged the boy and looked at him in happiness.

The boy stood awkward, ensconced within her arms. He felt embarrassed and fidgeted. Bulbul looked on in wonder at the ethereal vision that the lady of the house presented. Mala looked on at the tableau and cleared her throat in a rush, "Sorry malkin. The husband walked off this morning and we did not know where to look for him. This is the first time this has happened and I had no other option but to bring them here. Children, wish aunty Namaste*."

The children obediently folded their hands together in the traditional greeting. Monika looked at Madan and enquired excitedly, "Do you remember me beta?" Madan brow furrowed in response and he looked at his mother for help. Mala butted in and said, "but malkin, he was only two years old at the time. I don't think he would remember the incident well enough."

"I don't think so Mala. How can Madan forget Esther aunty? We spent a whole month looking into each other's faces."

Turning to look at Bulbul, she said, "You had not come into this world at the time dear child, but look how sweet you have turned out to be, same as your mother." Bulbul smiled happily at this. The compliment delighted her.

Monika bent to scoop the youngest in her arms and deposit him on the sofa in front of the TV before switching on a popular cartoon channel. An ecstatic duo rushed to sit next to their sibling and presently the three sat transfixed as they watched the popular episode of *Maya and the kingdom of the giant Elks* that was currently trending on the playlist. Once the children settled down, Mala rushed into the kitchen to begin her work but Monika's voice stopped her. "Not today, Mala. You have brought your precious children here, to my home. So, you are technically off duty. Sit back, and watch me cook something special for them." Mala complied in happiness and sat down.

Monika in the meantime, broke six eggs into a bowl, whisked them until they turned fluffy and proceeded to add chopped bell peppers, onions, and a dash of black pepper powder. She switched on both gas burners simultaneously and placed two flat pans on them. Once they were heated, she brushed their surface with oil and poured the mixture and sprinkled salt on top. Finally, she reduced the flame and covered both pans. While the omlettes were cooking, she boiled some milk and added a few spoons of sugar and rose essence. They were poured into two tall glasses. The little one would have to be fed by Mala. Next, she removed the covers from the pan and expertly flipped the omlettes. The kitchen was soon filled with the pleasant aroma of eggs being cooked. Switching off the heat, a layer of grated cheese was sprinkled on the surface and folded in half. The cheese would soon turn soft and gooey as the warmth from the just-cooked omlette seeped through. They were halved, placed on a plate and served. Mala was given a smaller portion which was meant to feed little Sheru. Placing him on her lap with a deftness born of experience, Mala allowed him to take small bites of the still warm food. The children sat absorbed, glued to the screen and ate without pause. They were hungry and Monika felt her heart constrict as she watched them.

The boy Madan was two when aunty Sandra had taken the fall. He had shifted loyalties and turned into Esther's constant companion, hardly leaving the old lady's bedside. Who was to know that circumstances would change all of a sudden leading to a virtual parting of ways for all concerned. All that it took was one instance, for events to take a different route. Upturn for some and otherwise for the rest. Life was so unpredictable. Never would one episode be the same as the others. To survive, you had to constantly be on the watch.

Mala's observation turned out to be accurate as Preet turned into a regular visitor and Esther herself became aware of the reason behind his visits. Philipa remained unaware of the latest development and carried on with her work and her energetic disposition therefore, remained unchanged. Aunty Sandra began to steadily improve although she remained confined to her bed. Very soon, it was only Madan and Mala, who stayed by her bedside to maintain their silent vigil. Esther and Preet spent hours in the garden and it was evident that they were serious about each other. Melvin was forgotten and so was Philipa. Mala and aunty Sandra knew that once Philipa got wind of the situation, all hell would break loose.

It did, just as she predicted. And how did Mala come to know all of this you may wonder?

Well, aunty Sandra's son Hank was stationed in Portugal and he called to say that he would make arrangements to transfer his mother back to where he stayed within a few weeks. The paperwork was being processed and so, the house they were in, would have to be evacuated upon his arrival. It would be listed on the property market and the brokers informed.

Meanwhile, the office was abuzz with rumors of a linkup between Esther and Preet. Philipa has been sidelined by two of her closest companions and that, did not go down well with her. She had an ugly spat with Preet and a blazing row with Esther. Aunty Sandra and Mala remained mute spectators and things twisted out of control when Philipa called Esther's parents to inform them that their girl was involved with a man who did not belong to their community. Soon, all hell broke loose on Preet's side of the family as well since he hailed from a culturally rooted north Indian family. Philipa walked out of their lives without believing a word of what Esther had to say. She has been wronged but it was never intentional, argued Esther passionately. She never made the first move. This was not planned. She did not want their beautiful friendship to be relegated to a far corner. It was Philipa she owed everything after all. But things changed. The animosity enveloped them from all quarters.

Esther and Preet were forced to move. Move away from Mumbai. To a place far, far away where they could live undisturbed. And that was how Mala met them once again. On a speeding train. The Mumbai-Mangalore express. A heavily pregnant Mala, her husband and Madan had caught the same train and were sitting in the unreserved compartment bound for the unknown. It was learnt that Prasad has been borrowing money from almost all the jhopdis while Mala was away at work and the shanty collectively took up arms against the family. Fleeing from them in the dead of night with not a penny to their name save for the clothes they wore, the family travelled in the hope of a future away from the hell that had been created. It was when Prasad alighted at one of the stations to fill their bottle with water that Esther caught sight of him and demanded Preet meet him and enquire the reason for his being there. Where was his family? Has he abandoned them? She would personally wring his neck if he abandoned Mala and Madan and was plotting to try his luck elsewhere. His good fortune would end then and there if that was the case. Esther would not hesitate to abandon Preet since her affection for Mala and her son went beyond reason. Their bond was special. She knew them before she met Preet and they were part of her life now. It was with relief that Preet conveyed the good news to her. And so, the group reunited once again and Preet bought additional tickets for all of them.

After much deliberation, they decided to disembark at the Thiruvananthapuram station where an old friend of her family, Sharada aunty stayed. The lady was considered to be a bit strange and it was known that she guarded her privacy quite fiercely. Esther reckoned that she could be trusted and would not give away their identity.

And that was how, Mala continued to work for Monika, the Esther of old and Sharada amma. Monika Esther D'Silva dropped the identity she was born with and adopted the new moniker, Monika Chadha. Preet decided to revert to his former name Pritam. Preet, as opposed to Pritam Chadha sounded overly casual and they needed a salve to soothe the ache. The responsibilities that they needed to face up ahead would have to match the personalities.

Mala gently deposited the little one on the sofa and picked up the plates. They were all wiped clean. Monika joined her and walked to the kitchen counter to prepare a cup of tea for the two of them.

Mala's heart brimmed with happiness. She looked at Monika and said, "you know malkin, there is a saying in my village. When you hurt someone, that comes to haunt you. I have experienced it myself and know it to be true." She paused and continued, "I felt that you should have opened up to Philipa didi regardless of your innocence in the beginning. It was your silence that hurt her the most."

Monika was quiet, the anguish evident in her eyes.

"Perhaps that is why your first-born was not meant to happen. But now, everything is clear. Pritam sir and you, will be blessed with a child soon enough. I can say with conviction that a new chapter is going to begin for the two of you."

***

Ever had a nail score a line across your cheek?
Felt it's caress from the soft mound under the eye
The pull on the skin, a gentle bite?
Red drops that ooze, gather and seep
A love-hate emotion, it's complexities unexplained
Intense as the flow, peppered by the grimaces.

My terror was real. Never had I witnessed fear this way. Rage, anger, unbridled happiness were emotions I experienced in surplus since young. But never the horrors of what I was going through night after night. Weekends were a long-drawn exercise in pure exhaustion. I realized that the body was only a vehicle that was meant to be used. You were unaware of its design or the purpose it was intended for. I knew that love was not destined for me. I was too cold, calculating, obsessed with money and the comforts it provided but when I saw the pretty face, I was bowled over. Well, the fall was in place just about the time the pretty face arrived. It was a fell swoop. The mother making her appearance right before the son and the situation that followed pretty much had me in its grasp. And that, proved to be my undoing.

It was my fifth year at the Astrid hospital. After my vicious flaying of Sahaj, my notorious reputation preceded my looks. I was admired from afar but none dared approach me. I was in the meantime, blissfully unaware of the looks or gossip directed in my direction. My bank balance was climbing. I was free, independent, and living my life. I clothed my beautiful body in expensive garments. These were sourced from boutiques that were visited over the weekends. I washed my skin with the milk squeezed from almonds. I soaked my scalp in a mixture of cold compressed castor and virgin coconut oils. My luxurious hair remained the envy of many. I doused myself in branded perfumes and I reveled in the way I looked, felt and smelled. Nothing would induce me to clean my apartment or cook food that would cast a blight on the physical beauty that I carefully maintained to perfection. I had a lady coming in to cook the perfect Mangalorean seafood curries and biryani that I craved for while another dropped in to keep my place clean. I knew that I was the target of ridicule and envy of my colleagues but I cared for no one. If at all I was destined to get hitched, it would be with a successful person who was financially sound unlike the cash strapped episodes of my childhood.

On the issue of men, there was this M.D. bloke I had my eye on for a while but he was from a different community and the more I thought about it, the more convinced I was about future problems that would inevitably make an appearance, and regrettably any action along that line would have to be avoided. So, I considered it safe to wait for the perfect horoscope match. The wait had been long and lucky for me in my opinion since I was never in a hurry and rather enjoyed my freedom although the latest candidate's mother - Mrs. Anumayi, seemed to have taken a fancy to me. I did not pay attention to the details as always for when the time would come, it will be Rashi, yours truly, who would offer the final 'aye.'

My ruminations over a cup of coffee were sharply interrupted. Mahendran the lift boy-cum-attender, came up to me and requested that I move to the head nurses' cubicle. A patient awaited that required expert intervention. I was to minister to her ailments and provide balm to the irritable disposition. I remarked that this seemed to be a two-way package deal. With a sigh, I picked up the file from the nurse on duty and walked towards the treatment room.

Mrs. Anumayi sat perched on the treatment bed with a look of impatience on her face. She held her right arm gingerly and I walked up to her. Her stiff countenance and marked disapproval at my lackadaisical approach, amused me. Most of the elderly patients were under the impression that they were to be served; that all and sundry at the hospital were meant to be at their beck and call. The Doctors and specialists occupied the higher realms of their affection. These were the demi-gods that cured them of afflictions. Inferior mortals like us who occupied the next levels in the hierarchy, were not worth the badge. If the professionals had their way, a structured setup tailormade to suit every patients fancy could have panned out but it could be safely mentioned here that such ideas never came into being. Class was a state of mind and not affiliated to position, power or wealth. You were born with it. It was a kind of stamp you sported. Something that you wore with honor. You flaunted it with pride. It was not something that was created by another with the intent to demean or rob you of your fundamental right.

I repeated the words over and over in my mind as I felt the fierce gaze burning a trail over my face and body ending at my sensible shoes. This was a lady mind you and were it to be someone from the opposite gender, a leer would have accompanied the look. Perhaps a suggestive pinch would have followed it as well? Ah well, these were minor flaws in a profession that so far offered me umpteen advantages.

I checked the woman's shoulder and tried to lift her arms. She responded with a painful yelp. This, was a frozen shoulder. A common enough problem that plagued most women her age. I glanced at her file and took note of the doctor's observations. This case would require a few visits for the joint to be workable and pain-free.

After the first two visits, the mockery and impatience gradually reduced. Perhaps the lady sensed the release and a gradual improvement in muscle tension was noted. The third visit had the lady attempting a polite smile. The mask finally cracked and her demeanor actually seemed presentable. I smiled in return. After a polite exchange, the lady went on to inform that her son Vinay - her only son was on the hunt for a bride.

I raised a brow. So, did she need a home bound therapist? My foot!

"It's not what you think Rashimol," she hastened to add.

I continued with the shoulder exercises and mobilization of the shoulder joints and, waited for her to continue which she did. Presently, she spoke, "My son is an aeronautical engineer and based in Bahrain. He has two elder siblings. One resides in Pune with her family and the other is a Bank employee and a widow. They have all taken a liking to you and approve of my choice."

My fingers stilled of their own accord. This conversation needed to be nipped in the bud. Frankly the lady seemed odd in the head. How pray, did two women come to like me without meeting me even once? Ridiculous!

Mrs. Anumayi continued blithely knowing that I would listen to her in all politeness. Politeness, my foot! On the contrary, I was seething like there was no tomorrow. I felt that the daft old lady was to be given a whack on the head.

"Vinay has been hunting for a suitable girl for ages. I think you would suit him well. For him, beauty is a consideration and you will be not be disappointed as far as his looks go."

"The stars have to match madam. My family insists on that," I felt my tongue working on its own in horror. What was wrong with me? I certainly did not want to let go of my comfortable position. As for leaving the country, that, had never been an option either. I could have held on to that fool Sahaj in that case or even the well-mannered dermatologist Dr. Shetty. Under Dr. Shetty's ministrations, my skin would glow in happiness, lifelong, for free. Perhaps the smile that crossed my face as a result of my musings, conveyed a misplaced sense of eagerness to the lady. She looked me over in her thoroughly ascertaining gaze and remarked that our stars seemed suitable enough and fell silent. I was glad of the quiet. Why did I feel a frisson of unease at her silence? Later, as she prepared to leave, I was asked for the address to my parent's home. She would take up the issue of a possible marital connection directly with them. Why, oh, why did I not clamp down on my feeling right then? My antenna had rung out a warning and I for once, did not heed the alarm. The clanging numbed my brain perhaps? For once, I ignored something that just didn't seem right even though I could not come up with a plausible reason for the dislike.

The thing with instinct is that, it's a silent invasion that rises up and blots out every other sensation in you. Something like a heavy truck mowing you down? I guess most people in love feel this way. One's sense of perception turns cloudy and you function within a dense fog. How you spend the rest of your day or days remains a distant memory. You float through time, the minutes ticking away slowly as if you are trapped in a dreamlike state. Your body functions seem normal yet, it isn't. Your thought processes enter a dim state and your ruminations take on a wispy form, immaterial and illogical they are yet, in your eyes, nothing else could make perfect sense. You live in a make-believe world; a realm that similar persons inhabit for a temporary period and the colors and feel of the place seem like nothing you have ever experienced. It is akin to floating on a marijuana induced state that lifts you to a higher level and the euphoria persists with the result that you tend to believe in miracles one of which, is happening within you, right that instant.

Oh, I had fallen in love alright. Except that, there was no man involved here as yet. It was the idea I had fallen in love with. Soon, I would be gaining something I had been hankering for and that, would keep me safe and sound, within my very own cocoon. The idea of a secure life coupled with the accessories most others lusted for were falling into my lap just as I wished for. I wanted to waltz right there in happiness.

Of course, Sharadamma and her husband would give out their approval. Which self-respecting parent wouldn't? Given the ferociousness with which my mother counted out her pennies and secreted them away in her bank account was proof enough. Going by Mrs. Anumayi's account, if the stars did match, then they would waltz with me. I had to wait for a week during which time, everything would be fixed and wrapped up. Oh, I was a changed person alright. My antagonism evaporated ever since the expectation level broke through and good news finally seemed to come my way.

After three days, the call came through but not in the vein that was expected. Sharadamma did not seem her usual self. I was concerned with the tone and tenor of her voice. She was not one to beat around the bush and came to the point right away. "Are you ok with this proposal Rashi? I do not feel good about it."

I felt my pulse race as I stammered, "Maa, you have been on the lookout for more than three years. I am assuming that the horoscopes match which is why you called?"

There was a brief silence. Her reply stunned me. "I feel disturbed Rashi. Somehow, this seems to smack of something rotten. The lady seems okay enough. You are not going to live with her anyway. But my gut feel tells me that this is not the right thing for you. Let's just chuck this. Something better will come up for sure."

I felt my heart plummet. This was outright rejection based upon a feeling. I sensed this earlier but had stifled it and let myself get carried away. Well, whatever was troubling this mother might be for the best. I managed a weak hmm in reply and ended the call. The sensation of defeat hung heavy on me. I had clung on to something insipid and that evaporated in no time. I had no good friends here at the hospital. Mandy and Pranauti were busy with their families. Our bond would not withstand the test of time. We were not reckless students anymore. I was thus left to my own defenses. Rushing to the washroom, I bawled for over half an hour and sat on the toilet bowl. My face was flushed, eyelids swollen and hair, mussed up. But what did I care? My dream fizzled away just when I was about to embark on a colorful ride. I was in despair and moaned in pain. There was a polite knock on the door.

A muffled voice called out, "Are you ok dear?"

The voice seemed concerned but I felt the rage boil over. "Go away. You effing piece of trash. Mind your own effing business."

The adjoining toilet flushed and a door creaked. Sounds of the tap water gurgling as a pair of hands were being washed was heard. Presently the main door of the washroom closed and silence was restored.

I inspected my nails and let the tears drip. Presently, I stood up and decided to move out. I needed a cup of strong coffee to revive my spirits and a movie later in the day. I would be fine by tomorrow. Rashi baby needed a jolt like this at times to shake herself out of her complacency. Men be damned. Mother-in-law be damned. Rashi and A.E suited each other. They could keep each other company. Thank the stars for her non-monotonous job. Not one case was the same as the other. Every individual responded towards their grievances in a unique manner. Being occupied in the line of duty therefore, was a given. She planned on sticking around until something interesting enough came her way!

***

Vinitha met Ammu in the summer of 2016. Now, who on earth are Vinitha and Ammu, you might wonder? Patience dear reader. Let's read through what Vinitha wants to convey shall we? The entrance of the two here, at this point of time is all interconnected I assure you. Let us try and connect the dots and unravel a few other situations that lead to the actual storyline. So, shall we begin?

Ammu was the friend of a common friend. I (that's me, Vinitha) had a select circle of friends but had heard about the newcomer (Ammu) from the time she came to stay in the building with her husband. We hit it off the first time we met. I thought that Ammu was funny. Her manner of conversing was direct and to the point. She was not flippant. On the contrary.

The limp was next. I noticed that it was quite pronounced. She had discerned the direction of my gaze. Her left leg dragged a bit and the weight of her body was placed on her right leg. I speculated on the gait. Perhaps it was something that was associated with her birth? I had a friend in school, who was born with a deformed left foot. It was polio that had dealt the cruel blow. But Vidya had been defiant and came out tops. She was now a senior officer in the Indian postal department.

Ammu was childless, confirmed our common friend. She was in her early forties and did not seem keen on having children. We stopped our chatter the minute she entered the room. Accepting a plate of Rasmalai from our favorite joint Bikanerwalas, she took her place beside us. Over the shared plate of happiness, we swapped stories of persons living within our apartment. I have been a resident of Green lake Apartment for long but Ammu seemed to have noted down all the oddities associated with most individuals. One other thing I noticed about her was the keen sense of observation and shrewd character appraisal.*

I conjectured that I had been hung and quartered in her estimation. So, I deliberated on asking her opinion as to what she understood about me, Vinitha. That I aspired to write my way through life, was a known fact. Our common friend had been kind enough to provide her all the details. Ammu also knew that I had a son and he was on his way towards completion of high school. In my spare time, I focused on being mentor and guide to a child. He was mildly challenged and I persevered in giving him tasks that would guide and stimulate him which would in turn, lead to his betterment. It was a pleasant hour that we spent, laughing and talking about common topics. Rather reluctantly, we had to part ways. Cooking and other household tasks had to be individually attended to. Moreover, it was nearing time for the kids to be back from school and we would be individually swamped. Ammu smiled and listened to our lamentations and bid us a gentle goodbye.

We met at the same venue a couple of times by which time, I had taken a liking for the lady. Her countenance glowed but it was the expression in her eyes, a sort of guard, that I noted. There seemed to be something lurking behind the veil. She had a rigid hold on herself. Of that, I was sure. Yet, we did not attempt to connect further. Nothing materialized beyond our common visits.

It was only after a few months when our mutual friend decided to shift to a newer apartment, that we began to associate with each other on a personal basis. The calls became frequent and she began to visit me once every week. I found her to be kind and considerate although quiet on occasions. She began to open up to me and I listened. I was keen to know what made her tick and it seemed that she had a well of experiences submerged within her. Most of them, I have described in detail starting from the beginning. But these were nothing compared to what she would confide and share, once the bond had been established. I was her elder sister, she said. A didi from another mother. She knew that I would watch out for her even though she did not wish for it. Her faith in humanity had eroded yet, here she was, a sea of strength and as pliable and functional as a bamboo stalk. She seemed stronger and although the scars were invisible, they still showed if one looked closely enough.

I vividly recall the day time stood still. It was as if two souls merged as one. Her anguish became my anguish. Her tears ran copiously through my eyes. I wrung my hands and winced as I felt the enormity of what was being revealed to me. The morning passed by in a haze and household duties were cast away without a thought. I longed to enfold this woman within my arms… to offer her comfort but words escaped me. I sat stock still as the enormity of the experiences bore down heavily upon me. This was beyond barbarism. Sadistic voyeurism within the four walls of a home was not an option regular people would choose to undergo. No one picked up a pretty little doll that would be malleable enough to withstand the horrors inflicted under the guise of acquiring pleasure unless you had the intent to do so. Sensations in this case, were to be the guidelines that would be followed by the giver and the receiver, both in this case, were on the same side. A heavenly union between two souls, one misguided, and the other doomed would occur with the result that cessation of mind functioning occurred. A dysfunctional life emerged in its wake. And the torment that was endured, isolated and submerged whatever pieces floated in its wake.

Mrs. Anumayi returned after two weeks. The pain in her shoulder reemerged and she was in agony. This was a common grouse that diabetic patients underwent. They often suffered from sleep deprivation plus lying on the affected side led to excruciating pain. The patient had been suffering from emotional and psychological problems compounded with the calling off of her sons' impending engagement. Her condition was further aggravated by the cessation of the exercises that she had to do on a regular basis following which, a gradual reduction in symptoms would have been noticed. In addition, the lady also wanted to plead with Rashi to reconsider her decision. The required treatment for her medical condition seemed to be the best approach. Her debilitative condition was genuine in any case.

Recognizing the intent, Rashi had given her the silent treatment and applied the hot gel pack to the affected area while the lady continued to howl and moan. Next, she went ahead with mobilization of the joints. These were a range of motion exercises that were undertaken in degrees in concurrence with the patient's pain threshold level. On one such occasion, the lady had grown rebellious and shrugged away Rashi's hand to which she coaxed in a half-threatening tone, "Mrs. Anumayi, please cooperate. You will have to undergo surgery if you refuse to exercise."

The formal use of her name had thrown the old lady off guard. "Pain management of this condition rests solely in your hands. There is no permanent cure and since your condition is very severe, it may take six months to a year for the symptoms to be cured. Even then, there is no guarantee that the symptoms will disappear. So, you have to decide how you want to go about this."

The firm tone coupled with the somber message elicited the requisite response. If she was expecting sympathy then she was in for a surprise. This was not Rashi's future mother-in-law that was being spoken to, was it? This was a patient who had requested treatment courtesy the fool of an orthopaedician - Dr. Murugan who had been swayed by her

Walk Away

entreaties. Rashi felt the urge to spank the lady. Curtailing her irritation, she gestured for her patient to arise. Picking up the warmed gel pack from its station, she placed it on the affected area in silence.

Mrs. Anumayi suitably chastened, stayed quiet for a while. Rashi gathered that she was plucking up the courage to start afresh. Timidly, she ventured, "Vinay will be here next month. He's been given four weeks of leave. I shudder just thinking about what I am to convey to him. He has set his sights on you my dear. I have been raving about you to my daughters as well. Then, your mother happened."

[So far, I have been visualizing the situation by placing myself in Rashi's shoes just like one often does during a story telling session or a theatrical video. But then, personal narratives are done best when recounted by the said person. Here, I was only a square peg within the round hole and a mute spectator to boot. I had to switch sides and allow Rashi to speak. This was her story after all.]

Looking at the woman's sharp eyes, I said, "My mother decides what is to be done with my life. For the moment, I have only one pressing concern. My career and my future. I wish to do justice to that. Therefore, kindly do not include me in your sons' personal wishlist. I'm sure that he will have a long line of suitable girls waiting to pluck him out of your arms since you swear by his eligibility."

"Rashimol, you don't know him," Mrs. Anumayi's hand had shot out and held the arm that ministered to her condition. I noticed a sweat bead roll from her temple to her jawline. Odd. The room was air conditioned. Yet, the lady seemed to be disturbed.

"Whatever Vinay decides, will be his to take. I know him well. He fancies you and will refuse to meet anyone other than you."

My eyebrows shot up at this. This guy seemed to have a sore head. Perhaps Sharadamma was right after all. Something did not sit right here. I could be an ugly wench for all you know. How could an unknown guy fall for someone by simply relying on a description provided by the mother?

"I sent him your picture. The broker was kind enough to provide me with a copy," was the sly response.

I zeroed in on Panicker uncle, our friendly neighbor-cum-broker.

The man had to be issued a dressing down. The lady had easily persuaded him and I was to bear the brunt of that erroneous decision. Sigh.

"Mrs. Anumayi, Your session has come to an end. I need to visit my colleague for a bit." I was eager to avoid the incessant head wringing. Once was enough.

"No, Rashimol, please listen to me. He will not take a 'no' as answer. You have not understood the situation well enough," --- her voice ended in a whimper.

Both mother and son seemed to be nutcases. What kind of marriages rolled down the aisle this way? The lady seemed cantankerous and obstinate. Her lower lip was beginning to jut out. Sulky huh? This fixation had me worried. A mother and son were targeting me like I was some kind of choice goods. I walked to the door and politely held it open indicating that the time had come for her to leave. The woman walked out with her head held high. Silly old coot, I thought. Coming in here and dangling her son like he was a trophy to be treasured. I planned to visit Dr. Murugan right away and shift the lady's forthcoming visit to Reena, my colleague who worked on alternate days.

There was a pause in the narration as I (Vinitha) suddenly developed a nagging headache. Offering an apology, I rushed to get an aspirin.

"So, you threw Vinay off the tracks is that it?" I asked on my return. Ammu was just getting warmed up. She was taking her time to come to the point. My patience was running out and I was eager to hear the rest.

"No," was the calm reply. "Vinay was my first husband. I married him after all." I coughed and spluttered as I searched for adequate words to respond. "He was persistent and the old woman was right. After a while, I simply gave in."

Vinay weds Rashi.

The happily ever after that was never meant to be.

***

Walk Away

Our meetings were sporadic after the shocker. I was immersed in my world and so was she. We often called and exchanged recipes. My son was the designated courier. We would send him back and forth with portions of food that came right off the stovetop. The two of us were foodies and we developed a great affection for each other. But that's where the similarities ended.

Ammu was a terrible homemaker and afflicted with a high degree of OCD. Although the claim of being ultra-efficient cleanliness-wise was pronounced ever so often, I found her living room cluttered with yet-to-be-folded clothes and knick-knacks. Their altar was choc-a-block with deities and pictures of all faiths and the dining table was cluttered with pickle bottles, crispy snack items and packets of all shapes and sizes. My goading and sarcastic remarks were endured but that was that. Perhaps she sank into bouts of lopsidedness. Her present companion was devoted but he was a workaholic and had his fair share of troubles on the career front.

After a good period of time passed by, I decided to take the bull by the horns and went down the lift to visit her flat below. My knocks and ringing of the bell went unanswered and I turned to leave by which time, I heard the key turning in the lock. Ammu stood watching me with an impish smile. She was pleased to see me I gathered. The moment I entered the tiny passage, she proceeded to lock the door and secure it with a latch and a chain-link for good measure. This amused me, for the apartment we lived in, was known to be a safe haven for families. The watchmen that manned the building, were well equipped to tackle any situation dire or otherwise. The measures that Ammu was taking therefore, seemed quite unnecessary.

"Precautions," was her hushed response.

I waited for her to spell out what she meant by that, in detail.

"I am jittery by nature and Ajin made sure that everything is secured just so, I feel safe."

Ahh.

That explained the skittish glances and hesitancy in conversing. My heart went out to her. Rashi emerged from being a stubborn, hot headed young girl to an independent career woman and finally, this mangled self that had sunk to the lowest level in the ladder of self-esteem.

The rise, I noted, was on its way. Ajin insisted on calling her Ammu in deference to her wishes and to erase a past that tormented her. The two were restless souls and bound to each other in a way they had not known existed. Both had been hurt. The damage was huge yet they now had each other for comfort. Sharadamma passed into oblivion a long time ago and all that was left by way of a family was her father and her brother along with his fledgling family. They were staying on the other side of town and offered no comfort by way of reassurances as a mother would. But family was family and Ammu was happy that she could lean on them when the tiredness seeped in.

Those occasions were rare, she amended hastily upon catching the look in my eye. For I was of the opinion that one had to handle one's troubles with a resolute air and utter lack of dependency on one's family members. They had grown their wings and our role was to let them be so that they could fly. Burdening them with oppressive thoughts would only pull them down and slow their flight thereby causing friction.

"I had this angst towards my mother while growing up. But somehow, all that began to change. And as I changed, our home seemed to bloom. Sharadamma began to smile. Quite often. Papa even began to render feeble jokes." Ammu reminisced with a smile as we sat on the sofa of her living room with a bowl of chips nestled between us.

"In hindsight, I now understand how maa struggled to maintain the balance."

"She was a strong woman," I agreed.

"Did you know, I have dreamt of leaving the nest and flying far away; where I cannot be traced. This was before Vinay of course. I tried to revive my plan post Vinay but here again, Sharadamma put a spanner in the works."

"How so?"

"Oh, she was adept at turning on the waterworks the minute she sensed it was essential. Plus, I became more receptive to her needs. My view of the world changed. After my stint at the hostel and the hospital, I have become a keen judge of character. It was in my personal space that my sense of judgement failed miserably."

I did not know what to say. She was right and we both knew it. I could only offer a shoulder that she could lean on. She had forgotten to trust and I was all she had. Ammu would not cry, I knew. She had mastered the art of bottling all of her emotions and through the sharing of her deepest fears and secrets, I was granted privy to her soul.

Oh, and by the way, let me tell you that she has been the one to suggest that I write down her life story; whatever has been recounted thus far, in a befitting manner. I was taken aback at the generous offer. Let me tell you that this side of her, was never confided to anyone other than yours truly and now of course, you, dear reader. It is therefore, my responsibility to construct a suitable plot befitting the events that occurred in the life of this brave, remarkable woman.

Had her mother gotten a whiff of what went wrong…. an iota of what her daughter had gone through, I believe, she would have turned into Kannagi - the fiery one who created hell on earth in memory of her late husband. Only here, the mother would have consigned the entire family of devils to ashes.

Ammu knew and feared this. And so, she kept mum. Hence, I was the only door that was allowed a preview of what went wrong and how. Ajin knew of course. The man had a heart of gold. Fiery temper notwithstanding, his thoughts and actions were way beyond the regular male temperament. All credits should go towards his upbringing in this case. And Ammu felt all the more secure due to this.

Now, the repercussions of letting Sharadamma in on her secrets would have shattered both father and sibling. They would turn into ruthless demons. She has endured one and was not keen in generating two more in its place. What could sprout in its aftermath was an inconceivable thought. Societal influences were a burden that cast its malevolence in an everlasting shadow. A deep-rooted malice that thrived and functioned on the alternative. And Ammu would become a prey to its rigor. A helpless one. She has broken out of the steel mesh that enfolded her for more than a year. The scars dented her personality to such an extent that she thought recovery was impossible. But she had come through the maze and walked out of it. She disallowed counsellors in helping her with the healing. She would do it on her own. And Ajin would be her silent support.

It was later that someone had made her appearance upon whom she would place her trust. Ammu had picked me to be the recipient of the purge. I would listen she knew, and understand. And I would shout out her story from the rooftops to the entire world. The objective was simple; there were more out there. Broken ones like her. And they needed to know that all was not lost. Hope was a solid thing. Choosing to fight back was possible. Fighting to get a grip on life without breaking was achievable. Vengeance need not be an option. That was a destructive mindset. To go on was possible. And by disproving everything that was meant to be, would usher in the change.

Choices tend to overkill.
They abandon-
Just when you reach out
Inch by inch
Towards that pinprick. Of light
To be secured
Within your bosom.

Groping through
Mind-numbing and the messy,
Those ever-tightening inward loops
That spews out finite sparks,
Release was a heady rush-
An elixir that coursed through.

Choices tend to overkill
They can be undone too.

***

Walk Away

Sharada overthought these days. Her powers of reasoning seemed to have deserted her. She felt that she was losing purpose in some way. Perhaps having achieved everything that a normal soul would have found easier to obtain, the constant planning and looking over the shoulder had taken its toll. Her journey had been strenuous. The amount of focus and determination it took to remain charged for a very long time had robbed her of her vitality. These days she spent a lot of time praying. Her concept of the divine had strengthened and she willed that her family live safe and healthy lives. She would guard their welfare with every ounce of her breath but after she was gone, what was to happen? She needed them to stay strong just like she had been when young. Her concern was chiefly towards Rashi but luckily, her girl had abandoned the resentment that had been harbored towards her. She was a sensible one, she thought in all fondness.

Working her way after securing a seat in the College of Medicine in Mangalore and being away from home for five long years was no mean feat. Visits to the home happened once a year and Sharada missed her able daughter's presence. She has been asked to refrain from travelling herself as it would worsen her condition and so, she pushed Ramakrishnan to act as her emissary. The good man would acquiesce in silence and return after four or five days. Sharada would in the meantime, keep herself appraised of her daughter's progress via. the phone.

Rashi had by now understood the seriousness of her condition and tamped down on her hostile mood. She was seeing a lot of the outside world and that widened her perspective towards life in general. Sharada on her part, was uneasy with the appearance of the roommates that had clung on to Rashi like leeches. The two were unbridled hags in her opinion and painted the town red with their wild escapades. Fortunately, her Rashi was quite unlike them although she was sure that she might have been subject to temptation by the indecent duo. It went on to speak volumes about the families they were part of. Poor Ramakrishnan was mercilessly trolled as 'Hitler' for being present at the venue on most occasions. Her man was only being obedient. What he spoke or how he reacted, was solely at her behest and hopefully, that would deter the wild duo from meddling in the affairs of their precious daughter.

Once, Rashi suggested that her father not visit her very often as she was being made the butt of jokes but the mother insisted. What Sharadamma asked for, she would ultimately receive, was their resigned conclusion. It was only when Rashi graduated and got herself employed at the Astrid Hospital that her vigilant mother finally relaxed. Ramakrishnan also felt that his duties could now be curtailed and mentioned as much. He was therefore, free to do what he pleased.

Mala's duties were now confined to cleaning and dusting. Sharada and her husband had teamed up and together, they planned meals and trips to temples, visited their relatives and settled into a routine that was quite systematic. Monika rarely visited them as she had the welfare of her two young children to look into plus a burgeoning business that catered to a section of interested buyers. Homegrown plants at a fraction of the cost were garnering itself a sizeable market. Mala's burden at both the houses had been greatly lessened although her work schedule remained the same. Her son had expressly forbidden her to work anywhere except the two houses that was dear to him too. Madan was now a part of the transport section of a huge conglomerate and drove one of the company cars. His job was to ferry the employees from their place of residence and back. Life turned out to be good despite the initial hiccups. He wished to keep his maa free from hardships and let her live her life as she wished. She has been burdened with so much since she could remember and now, all he wanted was for her to be at peace and look upon life in happiness.

Mala was planning to visit Bulbul's family the following day. Prasad would be at home and act as a lookout for Sheru, their youngest one. Sheru was a lion heart for real and the father was morbidly afraid of him. He attended the local polytechnic and planned to open his own mobile and electronics repair shop once he graduated. Sheru would keep both house and her husband in place until she returned. Bulbul was expecting her second child and Mala had a few gifts to be given away both to the in-laws and her son-in-law. It was part of their tradition. This would also ensure that her daughter would be taken care of until the time she visited her parent's home for the delivery. Mala doted on her grandson and hoped to spend an entertaining three days with the family. Madan arranged a cab to pick and drop her. It was a relief to be able to travel in the comfort of an a/c car. Gone were the days when she used to visit her village after travelling on top of a jampacked bus or train in the sweltering heat. Bulbul's house was a mere fifty kilometers away but the journey tired her out nevertheless. She bid adieu from Sharadamma's house and walked in the direction of her small two roomed home. Amma's house seemed to have achieved an aura of piety. The effect was unsurprising since she was totally committed to her poojas and rituals. The level of dedication remained unwavering as of old but lately, she seemed to lack the drive. There was a decrease in her physical functioning and secretly, she felt worried. She hoped that the malady, whatever it was, would disappear on its own. Clearing her mind of the uneasiness, Mala thought of her grandson and her lips curved in a smile.

Sharada watched her husband hack away at the weeds in their kitchen garden. The sprouts were beginning to rear their heads but never got a chance to flourish. Ramakrishnan was an expert at identifying the outsiders. They had a carefully cultivated area that was dedicated to a few essentials. The ubiquitous curry leaf plant and the omnipresent drumstick tree stood a few feet apart interspersed by the mint, coriander section and the fiery red chili of the south - the *kanthari*. Both the red and white varieties provided fodder for the dishes Sharada cooked. In another corner stood the sacred tulsi (holy basil) and pots of thyme. There was a neem and lemon tree up in the front and coconut and papaya trees lined the back wall. The pumpkin patch grew next to the drumstick tree and several tendrils latched on to its rough bark. They were beginning to flower and the couple expected a good harvest this season. Sharada continued to feel pensive and uneasy. The sudden arrival of the newcomers had thrown her insides into a tizzy.

Ramakrishnan was engrossed in his routine. His back and hands ached. He felt tired and sweaty. When would Sharada offer him a glass of lemonade?

His wife seemed unusually quiet and at a loss for words. When she hesitantly voiced out her reservations about the proposal, it did not come as a surprise. He had noticed the discomfort in her voice. The years had attuned his senses to the extent that the tiniest of change would put him on alert mode. She was advancing in age and he knew that the health issues would crop up. It was only a matter of time. But this one threw him off course.

Turning with care to rest on his haunches and face his wife of thirty odd years squarely in the eye, he countered, "What do you think?"

"Well, for one, I did not like the look in her eyes or her mannerisms. It reeked of freshly minted money and that is a singularly unattractive quality to look out for, while groom hunting."

"Why do you say that?" Ramakrishnan was intrigued and waited to hear his wife's viewpoint on the subject.

"You are financially deprived and then the money arrives. Suddenly you are the object of envy. Your lifestyle undergoes a sea change. The new house, cars, clothes, jewelry, bank balance and other material comforts provide an adequate cushion from the insecurities you have faced in life. The haughtiness in your demeanor makes its appearance.

That's the first sign. Since your son is the reason for the affluence, everything associated with him will be subjected to the minutest of scrutiny. All this was evident from the woman's mannerisms. Added to the fact that she took our 'supposed agreement' for granted. She thought I would kowtow to her and bow down in deference. Arrogant, classless, crass woman," ended Sharada in disgust.

"Oh…" was all Ramakrishnan could manage at the time. He had not sensed that something was amiss. The lady seemed polite and well-mannered but women are far too perceptive. And his Sharada could sniff out trouble from a distance.

"Our Rashi is getting on in age. I hope she was not enamored with all the sweet talk. This one just didn't look or feel right. And she was not accompanied by her husband. That did not look right to me either. When you are approaching a family for a possible union, all the members should be present and mutually agree on customs and other details. I smell something fishy. I did not like the mother at all."

The matter had thus been decided, hung and quartered. There would be no looking back. Ramakrishnan quietly went back to his weeding hoping that his wife would quit ruminating and make him a cold drink. The day was fairly sunny.

The phone call to her daughter had been made and the decision conveyed. Rashi seemed upset but accepted the verdict. Perhaps the time was not right. They had to wait awhile for the right man to come along. Sharada has promised to make up for things once a date was fixed. She hoped that her daughter trusted her instincts and went along gamely. That phony lady was not to be trusted.

She was right after all. Things did go out of hand. The crafty woman had plotted it all down to the T. The snare had been set and her daughter neatly baited.

Mrs. Anumayi's son Vinay, disembarked and took the first taxi out, to the hospital in search of Rashi. The sudden meeting left Rashi flustered. She was unprepared for the visit… taken off-guard. A handsome stranger stood before her with eyes that spoke volumes. At first, Rashi thought that the famed actor Kamalhaasan stood before her for real. The man had the sweetest countenance and radiated passion. As the nurses oohed and aahed, Rashi felt elation wash over her. This was manna that had dropped straight from the heavens to meet her. For the first time in her life, she felt tongue-tied and her brain had ceased to function.

After he left, Rashi deposited herself on a chair. Her legs felt dizzy and insides, warm and fuzzy. Her colleagues crowded around her and crowed in excitement. Their Rashi was finally getting hitched. She has turned into the surprise of the week. Her find has been a fantabulous one, they had to concede. The wait was long but the bait proved to be thrilling. There were excited giggles, whispers and gaiety pervading through the lounge. The arrival of the head nurse disbanded the group and everyone rushed to their stations in silence.

Rashi was enveloped in a haze of warmth as she dragged her leaden feet towards her room. The man's face refused to disappear from her mind. He was definitely loaded, good looking and best of all, he wanted her! Did she detect a gleam in his eyes as he looked at her? Her heartbeat quickened and her face flushed in happiness. Taking an hour off from work, she rushed to her regular salon to freshen up. Her hair and nails were in perfect condition. The eyebrows had to be tweaked a bit and a few stray hairs off her upper lip cleared and she was primed; ready for the evening meet. At five p.m. sharp, her mobile phone rang and she walked down the stairs from her room on the first floor, cleared the distance from the ground floor to the grand front doors of the hospital in a half-run and out, towards the gate.

Mr. Handsome stood waiting and the look in his eyes made her blush. She imagined herself to be swept away by the man of her dreams in an elegant white car and it all seemed to be coming true. Her mother's fears were unfounded. She would feel better once she met Vinay. Her daughter was in safe hands and she could rest easy.

***

PART II

Sometimes the colors spun.
Wildly careening, as though out of control.
Blurry they were, mingled with the tears.
Helpless, rage infused
Shiny and slick,
Splashes of it seeped onto tongue.
Tasting of bitterness and raw despair.

Purple bruised ache; that bloomed mild orange
Apathy disconnected; melding into shades of red.
Gradual mottling into sickly shameful green,
Refuge found in the yellow, as scars appeared
And reappeared.
One among many, of the visible.
Connecting fist. Dull thumps. Routine thwacks.

Hair pulled, roots uprooted, soul blanching...
Veined exhaustion, slow numbness
Morbid fascination exchanged for irreverence
Giving in was a reality.
For a life that had been given.
The colors - they were unceasing
In their arrival and, aftermath.

THE DARK PHASE

"You are mine." She heard him speak. The words had echoed within the dim recesses of her mind. "Henceforth, you are to be referred to as, Rashi Vinay. Any reference to your family is to be obliterated from your identity." Calm words belied the underlying threat. Rashi felt her step falter as she stood on the heavily decorated podium surrounded by her immediate family members.

June 1990. The A.L. Rajah auditorium where her lavish wedding was being held, was the cynosure of all eyes. Rashi's parents and brother were beaming in happiness. Strangely enough, she felt a part of her register the implications of the words uttered into her ears with a sense of horror.

Her mother registered the dip in expression with concern. She was doubly no, triply perceptive to her daughter's vacillating emotions. "What is it dear? Are you feeling alright?" Rashi squeezed her arm in

response and shook her head.

Not now maa.

Not here.

I may be mistaken but nothing should go wrong at this point of time.

The mother looked away suitably chastened and berated herself in silence. Maybe the thought of her dear daughter who would soon part from their midst had felt a twinge and she had caught on to that. Silly her. Flashing a wide smile at her future son-in-law, she stepped away from the dais to confer with her relatives on the upcoming ceremony.

A kilo of gold flashed like armor on the divine looking bride and Sharada glowed in pride. She had penny pinched and saved every bit so that they could stand tall among the family and revel in the glorious feel.

Soon, all too soon, that perfect dream had come crashing down and the flip side had shown its ugly side. Barely had they reached his house and the fatigue dispelled that the nightmare begun in earnest. The piercing scream that emanated from her throat had just been the beginning. She was pushed against the cotton bedspread and viciously mauled. This intrusion had been the red flag she sensed deep down. A relentless campaign that had plundered and looted every shred of her body, every fiber of her being. She was feasted upon; torn and bloodied, as the rampage went on and on and yet, she suffered through an excruciating existence for one simple reason - that her family remain in the dark and not know or hear of her agony.

How was she to explain the days that passed? What about the shame? Wouldn't the knowing glances mock her, day in and out?

She was to blame. She was sure of it.

She had sensed the change. The slipping of the façade.

The carefully cultured mask revealed itself on that fateful day and to her everlasting regret, she had willfully pushed the nagging doubt far, far away. Was it because of the portentous moment? What would have happened if she had stepped off the dais mere minutes before the tying of the thaali? Perhaps she attributed the moment to nervousness. She had observed the look of worry flit across her mother's face. Of the dreams that would come crashing down. She feared the ugly gossip that would follow, downing them all in shame. All that money and finery wasted on account of an uncommon whim.

Of course, Vinay's family would wallow in the sympathy. Sympathy fueled by pointers of hate towards the Kurup family - her family. She was known to be arrogant. Vinay was lucky to escape the dragnet of the shrew. Their community would have girls swarming over his good looks and plush job. He would not want for anything.

Coming to looks, he was a crowd puller. Heavy lashes framed a gaze that you could swoon over and his complexion was something to die for. But a monster clothed in the devil's garb was easy on the eye. They were known to lure you towards them with their magnetic smile and wily ways. And she had fallen for the charm like a sewer rat drawn to the deep dark alley that it inhabited and was being tormented for that one fatal error she had chosen to sidestep earlier. A flaw that pushed all the alarms of her system into red alert mode. Dear lord, she was being punished for something she has craved all her life. Was she being denied happiness for some fault of hers? All that her mother ever wanted, was for her to live in contentment. If she could have read her future in advance, wouldn't she have picked Sahaj over Vinay?

Ammu heaved a huge sigh and went silent and I (Vinitha) felt her distress. The muscles of my throat felt tight as I wearily got up to offer her a glass of buttermilk. She accepted it gratefully and drank the contents as if parched. Our thoughts overlapped and hearts beat together as one. She was reliving her harrowing past and I was experiencing the agony. The physical pain was unendurable but the trapped soul that beat out a far more agonized rhythm, what about that?

It took a week for the body to recover from the initial onslaught. The invasion had been quick, leaving her senseless for the rest of the afternoon. When she regained consciousness, the house seemed quiet. Rashi comprehended on the severity of the action. She was trained to spot and analyze on the outcome after all. The only difference this time was that, she was at the receiving end.

Perhaps it had been a one-off, she reasoned. The man might have gotten over excited. And she reacted like the frightened virgin she was. Rashi lifted her aching and sore body from the bed and hesitantly walked towards the door. The flowers that decorated the room had dried and a stale odor hung in the air. The room had not been swept clean was her surmise.

Stepping over the threshold of the room into a long verandah, she perceived a rather serious looking Mrs. Anumayi, now her mother-in-law, peering at her through her oversized spectacles. The slavish look of old disappeared and an aura of command enveloped the slight figure.

"Aah, you are awake," the steely glance gave her the once over. "Neeli," she hollered. "Where is the slowcoach when we need her the most?"

"You need to clean up first and have a good cup of tea." No offer of a chair for her to sit upon. This hag was the one who had simpered her way through her good offices once, mused Rashi in private.

"Where's Vinay?" queried Rashi of her mother-in-law. She did not care to respond to her statements. The casual tone stung and the old woman bristled.

"You are not to use his name henceforth." Two sets of glances collided with the hag backing down after an instant in reluctance. Rashi knew that it would not be for long. This would be a long-drawn battle, cautioned her A.E. She would have to turn into a veritable twin of Sharadamma. That would be the only way she could pin this piece of irrelevance to the wall. But Vinay? That was a potential minefield. She had to figure him out first. She hoped against hope that he would regain control of himself. She has been privy to the vagaries of human longing but never experienced the thrill of it. Hopefully, what happened with them the first time, would be a thing of the past.

It turned out that she was in the wrong once again. What seemed to be a slip and a fumble, pleasurable pastimes that endeared, turned out to be 547 days of sheer hell. Her body was ripped apart although the shell was intact. But that was just about it. The ogre had been ruthless. A phase of penitence would follow after satiation of the wild spell and the begging, pleading for forgiveness and abject despondency would shake her out, dredge her from the stupor. And the cycle would begin all over again. Repeat. Pause. Repeat. Thus, went the pattern. There was never a cessation to the routine.

Was this how marriages were meant to be? Was the agony part and parcel of the package and meant to last a lifetime?

Ammu mumbled the questions over and over as my head throbbed in pain. One glance at my fingers tightly gripping the edges of the table spurred her into action. I was reliving my friend's agony and she understood. I was escorted to the bedroom and gently deposited against the soft cushions where I succumbed; to the incoming tide.

My migraine had resurfaced and the feeling of disorientation stayed on for a while. I also found myself in the grip of a raging fever. My insides lashed out at the horrendous journey that a remarkable woman had managed to overcome. Was it possible that I was the only living person to hear of the harrowing account face to face? Ammu responded by telling me that Ajin - wonderful, wonderful man, was also in the loop. He was privy to all that she had endured. I mentally bowed down to this angel garbed in the form of a human. He was indeed the beacon who offered her hope. All he asked for in return, was love. Dual forms of the same thing, experienced by the same person and that was indeed a paradox life had meted out to Ammu.

My bond with my friend had been strengthened many times over. It was as though I was pre-assigned to be the blanket that she required from time to time. The outer glint flashed at times, scarred as it was but the shine was still there.

She had been mauled, stubbed with live cigarette butts, continually used on a must-have basis during the weekends and yet, deep down, she bore the relentless assault in grim silence. On one occasion, she was kicked and her lower back had borne the brunt of the assault following which, she slipped from the bed to land on her knee - the one that still bore the signs and would continue to do so until she departed from the confines of her physical self. Thus, was born the limp that had permanently marked her for life.

I heard the rage in her voice. Sensed the war between the sane and the not-sane. But the momentary pain in a premediated action would dull the senses and offer him respite which, she was unwilling to do so. She needed to hang on to the pain - both physical and emotional. It served as reminder.... just so that she would not fear its implications. She was trapped and nothing or no one could help her save her own self. So, she would not give in. Surrendering to the easiest course of action was not how she was primed to react. She would ensure that Vinay thought otherwise. That he had won over her in totality. By holding on in silence, she would ensure that she remained safe.... and alive. Her Sharadamma taught her that. Her mother had taught her well. She resolved to be strong and not reel under the unpleasantness life was dishing out. So, how would SHE do it? How would Sharadamma work her way out of this confinement? How was the monster to be outwitted?

She had to steel herself and be prepared for the flight. The myth of the much admired, well-heeled man with his minion had to be shattered and by God, she would work at it. She would wait for her chance until the way ahead was clear.

***

Ammu loved mambazha pulissery and mutton cooked in a thick gravy. King fish fry and crisp pappadams would round off our meal quite nicely. I had invited her over for a full day. The subject of her escape intrigued me. My partners were away on a fun trip. They understood. The writer in me was taking over. I was determined to recount her story. Shout it out from the rooftops so that people would hear; choose to keep their eyes and ears open, recognize potential signs that distressed or invited trouble and offer a shoulder to lean on for those who suffered. Of course, one cannot foresee or predict as to what would happen the very next instant but life has to go on. Situations have to be undergone regardless of the care one takes. We have to learn to give it our best shot.

The mutton had been marinated in a mix of thick yoghurt and assorted spices. I cleaned the pieces of fish and smeared a paste of my special masala on them. The rice had been washed, put into the rice cooker along with the required amount of water and the timer had been set. I proceeded to fry the pappadams in hot oil and as they puffed up, I strung them on a long steel rod that was designed for the purpose and after the excess oil on them dripped away, stored them in a stainless steel dabba.

Next, I deskinned the mangoes separating the yellow, fragrant skin from the succulent flesh. They were added into a pot with a little water, a teaspoon of red chili powder, salt, a pinch of turmeric and allowed to cook for ten minutes. Once the mango pieces turned soft, in went the ground paste of coconut, yoghurt, cumin and green chili and the contents were given a quick stir. Once the first few bubbles appeared and began to pop, I added the required salt, switched off the flame and readied the seasoning. In went two tablespoons of coconut oil, a teaspoon each of fenugreek seeds, mustard seeds, dry red chilies and curry leaves. The tempered mix is designed to bring out an exotic aroma that can make anyone swoon. After adding this to the mango mix, all that is required is a small piece of jaggery to even out the taste. Our mambazha pulissery was now ready and good to go.

I now paid attention to the mutton which was being pressure cooked to perfection. Taking a pan, I added whole spices; a bay leaf, two cloves, whole cardamom, powdered peppercorns, home-made garam masala powder, red chili powder, turmeric powder, ginger-garlic paste and finally, a whole lot of onions. Once the mix thickened and browned, in went the diced tomatoes. The succulent mutton pieces went in next. After ensuring that the concoction was simmering gently, it was checked for salt and finally, thick coconut milk was poured in. The gas was switched off and a bunch of fresh curry leaves were added after the pot was taken off the counter. To highlight the wow factor of the rich and flavorful gravy, a final handful of chopped coriander leaves was deftly blended in. I couldn't wait to tuck in and so, I changed into a set of fresh smelling clothes and waited for my friend to appear. Picturing the happy smile on her face, I grinned in anticipation. Our discussion was entering a dark phase. My offering would counter the unpleasantness. We had meandered together through an emotional abyss. It was time to take an objective look and reflect on the lessons learnt. Hope was always an arm's length away.

I offered an admiration-tinged salute to the iron lady I knew -Sharadamma. Scaling Mt. Everest seemed pretty trivial when compared to what she has achieved. As for her Rashi; well, she had crossed her bridges and was gamely holding on. If that was not worth a mention, then what was?

***

Sharadamma felt her heart constrict in anxiety. The palpitations were frequent. It was a sign. One that was designed to upset her balance. The worry ate at her and Ramakrishnan suffered as a consequence. Her instinct had been right. Something was constantly pinging in on her thoughts. Her courtesy call to Mrs. Anumayi had been a disaster just as she predicted. Rashi has not called home in two months and the lady was feigning innocence. Bahrain was thousands of kilometers away and this time, Hitler could not make the habitual trip to check on the situation. The lady's nonchalance had troubled and vexed Sharada.

Mala sensed the desolation the moment she entered the home and was surprised to see the man of the house morose and attached to the rocking chair, palmyra fan in hand. Amma was inside, she was informed… resting. Mala peeked into the bedroom and noted the

Walk Away

dispiritedness. Something seemed amiss. Was she sick? Bad news within the family perhaps? All of her queries were waved away. Sighing, she proceeded to clear the kitchen countertop of the clutter. The clutter was another sign that something was terribly wrong. The spotless kitchen had never been in such a disgraceful state before. With a speed born of experience, Mala worked for the best part of an hour and brought a semblance of order to the space she was familiar with. Broom in hand, she moved out into the courtyard and swept the area of the fallen leaves and flowers. She proceeded to sweep the sides of the house, moving like an automaton, her wrist flicking in precise, slick movements and the ground was gradually cleared and neatness restored. She picked out the flowers meant for the evening puja - *Nithya Kalyani** for the Gods, *white mandaram** for Shiva, a few red roses and hibiscus for the Goddesses and yellow marigolds for the altar. These, she placed inside the small room that were filled with pictures of the deities that Sharadamma worshipped. The flowers nestled inside a wide mouthed brass vessel and Mala paused for a moment to admire them.

Whatever is troubling the lady, please set it right *Mahadev*. Let her not suffer. She deserves better. Show her some compassion. Her devotion to you has been unflinching. Resolve her dilemma and set her free O Lord of Lords. Let her find happiness.

Mala felt the tears gather in her eyes and she dabbed at them with the ends of her sari. The good woman needed to be roused so that she would focus on the evening rituals. This mooning about wouldn't do. Mala shook her head determinedly and walked towards the room where the mistress lay, intent on rousing her. The slumber had to be shaken off.

"My Rashi's in some sort of trouble," moaned Sharada in a feeble voice.

So that was it.

Amma's intuitive gift was an unnecessary burden sometimes. Mala wished that her own mother been more receptive to her troubles. Life would have flown by easily in her case.

"You fret too much about her Sharadamma. She's a grown woman now. Well educated with a spine of steel that you taught her to have. How can she be in any form of trouble?" countered Mala although her mind quailed in uneasiness.

"You don't understand. Vinay's mother set my teeth on edge the first time we met. Then there was that one instant..." her voice trailed away as she puzzled over the moment. Rashi looked devastated. The radiant bride who dazzled all with her appearance seemed crushed; shaken by a realization. She had felt it deep down. There was something that the boy must have whispered to her. Sweet nothings would make any bride blush but this was not it. A grim foreboding had filled Sharada's heart and she wanted to know. But her lovely Rashi, her darling daughter had rushed to pacify her. Her glance had coaxed her into normalcy. She should have been coerced into voicing out whatever troubled her. Was her daughter paying a price for the error she committed?

"It has been months since she has called. We are unable to get in touch with her. Vinay is at his charming best when we call him. Says there is something wrong with her phone and that she has secured a senior position at the Bahrain General hospital. The salary is excellent, he has assured us. He seemed pleased about it too. Said she would call us soon. What does he mean by that?"

Mala blanched in fear. This seemed serious. She did not know how best to convince her mistress. Perhaps Monika di and Pritam sir could come over and speak to the two. Take them for a long drive and try to assuage them. They could also reach out to acquaintances or family members known to Rashi and try and make the connect. This was nothing like her Prasad's spineless behavior. Was Vinay as sinister as had been portrayed? Mala shivered inwardly and hoped that the situation did not seem as murky as indicated by Sharadamma. Reassuring her with words devoid of hope, Mala helped her shift focus on the impending puja while her insides churned. "Lord, save us from calamity. Place your hand on us. We need you now, more than ever."

***

Vinay prided himself on his looks. In fact, his complexion glowed every time he inspected himself in the mirror. Ammu's casual observation on avarice; that it goaded one to rack up on those acquisitions made me think. Made sense in her case though. This was like the leech that latched on and hung around, aware that it had everything to gain. The realization bloats the parasite beyond perception thereby helping it to bask in its reflection. For Vinay, Rashi was only an object that he desired to possess. A veritable, breathable human toy that acceded to all his demands without a squeak. Gone was the blustery approach. Such was the shadow of the devil's demands that she gradually forgot her true self.

The man was also a narcissist. Such was the importance placed on his appearance. Not just that, but every aspect of his development had been put in place that would exude an aura of perfection. He was an aircraft maintenance engineer and commanded a position that befitted his experience. Twice yearly trips to exotic locales meant that they made three breathtaking visits before the inevitable happened. Europe, Greece and Istanbul were accessed in levels of splendor that she had never experienced before.

Ground rules to be adhered to during the travel sessions included staying mum while exploring the locale, nil eye contact with any male passers-by except for the doting husband and enjoy the luxurious setting that she was privileged to be a part of. To add insult to injury, talks of an additional member that would soon grace their household began to creep into conversations.

What brought her out of the stupor she had sunk to Rashi could scant remember but one such subtle hint snapped her consciousness into alert mode. Perhaps it was her mother's prayer that helped her see the light. Her Sharadamma would have sensed her unhappiness. And from that minute onwards, Rashi began to think of the long flight towards freedom. The devil needed to be outwitted. She would enlist her colleague's help and start making plans.

The devil in the meantime remained oblivious to the awakening. His mind was tuned in on the obvious as always. Rashi contended that she would have to bear a few more slaps or kicks and the occasional burn mark to reach her goal. She did not have any of the local currencies with her. The ATM card allowing access to her salary was in his hands. She shopped for expensive designer wear that was paid for by the D.

Provisions for the house was bought by the D.

She was accompanied by him on every little trip.

She had no known friends that she could rely upon.

She talked to no one. Not one explicit detail of her personal life was shared with anyone and that included Priti.

But Priti the gynae had understood. She had noticed the covert marks, the wincing, the measured steps and labored breathing. Medical professionals are taught to be discreet. Hence, she stayed silent and watchful. Rashi knew that Priti knew but she offered her nothing. Not even a hint. But the two grew close. It was a strange relationship.

It was after the light flipped that Rashi made her approach. "Dr. Priti, I need help."

The urgency in the tone struck the lady as odd. They had always taken care to stay on neutral grounds. Carefully dropping the used syringe into the bin marked 'hazardous waste,' Dr. Priti turned to face her colleague and dear friend.

"Bol yaar. Mein tere liye kya kar sakti hoon?*"

Rashi looked away. After a slight pause she continued, "I need to get a key duplicated. Can you get it done in an hour's time?"

"Um. Well, I could give it to you the next day. Chalega*?"

"No, No, No," frantic hand gestures followed the agitated reply. "I need them within the hour, if not less. I cannot risk being discovered Doctor." Chest heaved and the dam broke. Muted sobs began in earnest.

The kind-hearted doctor was naturally alarmed. Bidding Rashi to sit, she rang her husband and conferred with him. Rashi had by then hunkered deep down into her chair and was weeping copiously. Something was seriously wrong. The girl had just returned from their third rendezvous and now this.

"Don't ask me anything Priti di. You best not know anything at all. Also let me tell you that I cannot pay you for this. I have no money to give you… for the moment. But I swear I shall pay you back… every penny of what I owe you."

The bastard. He was using her and eating up her earnings as well.

The lout had a cushy job and was handsome to boot but it seemed that he had never given this girl the happiness she deserved. Priti felt the bile rise up in her throat. Damn this unequal world. How could she help this woman? She couldn't call the cops. Neither could she give the support that the girl required.

The phone pinged and Priti glanced at it. Dharmesh, her husband was on his way. She reassured Rashi and signaled that she would be back soon. Rashi was to wait in her room until she returned. All she got was a mute nod in reply.

An hour later, Rashi entered her apartment. Both keys, duplicate and original, lay nestled under each of her breasts, snugly held by the elastic band of her bra. She would return the original key to its place once Vinay would get into the bathroom for his nightly wash.

Her A.E had risen and the stupor had vanished. It was she, her secret and sensible friend, who had harped on the importance of having a duplicate key that guarded the contents of a secret so shameful that no living soul was to know of it. The key opened into a small locker by their bedside and contained a camcorder plus an assorted set of tapes. These held scenes that were filmed by the D as he cavorted and scripted his fantasies the likes of which she never thought possible. Most of her wounds and burn marks were a direct result of these escapades. Her A.E. counseled her on carrying the stash with her as she made her escape and destroy them before she boarded the flight. The duplicate key had to be within her reach just for the same reason. Knowing how vengeful he could get, it didn't make sense in leaving them behind for him to use them to coerce and if that failed, public-shame her.

The next goal was to procure a ticket that would take her home. Dr. Priti would facilitate that for her. She would walk away from the hospital, hail a taxi, enter the airport, trash the tapes and camcorder and board her flight. Her expensive clothes, collection of sleek shoes, perfumes, makeup kits and the hard-earned money she had stashed in the bank, she would walk away from them all.... without a backward glance.

Rashi stealthily replaced the original key in its slot. Her passport was in the locker as well. The conceited oaf was under the impression that she lacked a brain. On the contrary, Rashi was on a high. She would not give up without a fight. Walking into the kitchen, she opened the lid of a container that was used to store raw rice. Rashi folded the long sleeve of her nightdress and dug her hand deep until her fingers located a familiar strip placed at the bottom. This, she pulled out with a deftness borne of practice. Slipping out a tablet that lay nestled within its bubble, Rashi quickly gulped it down with a mouthful of water. The strip was once again placed deep within its resting place, tight and snug and, the lid of the container was replaced as before.

Relief washed over her. Another day, another crisis averted. Few more to go before the farce ended. The birth control pills were such a godsend. God knows, she did not want the freak to dote on his creation. To her, the thought was abhorrent, downright repulsive. She would not let the D gain an upper hand, no matter what. The stakes were too high here and she could not afford to fail.

***

The phone rang within the Pallikal residence and an anxious Sharada hastened to receive the call.

"Hello?" Breathless enquiry tried to mask rising eagerness.

There was a momentary clearing of throat and Sharada heard the clear voice speak in reply. "Good morning Didi. Monika here. How are you?"

Disappointment rose up and chest clenched in agitation.

"I… I have something cooking on the stove. Need to check it out. Can we talk later?"

"No, no don't hang up Didi. Please…."

The entreaty cut through Sharada's fog. She perceived the genuine reaching out.

"What is it, Monika? Ramakrishnan is waiting for his breakfast." The tone had gentled and Monika breathed a sigh of relief.

"I am paying a visit to our Patron Saint - St. George's Edapally church and the adjoining Kottaram Ganapathy temple soon after. Siya and Riya will be accompanying me. Pritam will be there of course."

Sharada knew what was coming. She had readied the refusal in advance but her dear friend forestalled her. Monika knew that Didi would refuse.

"The girls need to pay their monthly visit. Plus, we need to make a collective wish…" unfinished sentence hung heavy in the air, heavy in its implications.

"No, I cannot. Will not… not today…" Sharada's tone weakened. She did not wish to argue.

There was too much weighing in her mind of late. She needed to bring her daughter home. Back in their midst. The extra time spent away from her altar would delay the proceedings by even a few minutes and she could not bear the delay any longer.

A rising certainty had taken root in her thoughts that her child was suffering greatly and only her prayers could bring her out of the conflict she was entombed in. Not that she knew what it was and she did not wish to know but there was an element of risk involved in the attempt to reach out. Rashi would suffer greatly and the setback would be greater making it impossible for them to clear the way. Sanal was unaware of the dark thoughts that plagued her and rightly so, for he was a brash youth, filled with the arrogance of the young. His fledgling career took him away from home and he hardly kept in touch with them, the ones who doted on him and pandered to his every wish but the truth had not escaped his aging parents. They had known him for what he was. It had always been their daughter - the apple of their eyes that they constantly worried about.

Monika perceived the weakening of Didi's tone and emboldened, pushed ahead with her POA. "Didi listen, you have heard of St. George right? He's someone who grants you your wish if you reach out to him deeply enough and all you have to do, is to light a candle or two. Right behind the church is the Ganesha temple and we could watch the evening arti and ask him to remove all the obstacles that are in Rashi's way." There. She said it. Sharada stood immobile, shocked at what she had just heard. That fool Mala must have cooed everything to Monika and now this.

Slam.

The receiver was banged onto its holder with brute force and a fuming Sharada stomped in anger towards the kitchen.

Ramakrishnan watched this exchange in silence and quietly accompanied his wife whilst she cooked and laid the table. A smoldering Sharada was hard to accost and the good husband recognized the signs and symptoms of impending doom and so, he observed calm. As he ate in silence, drank his tea, offered to wash the dishes and cut up a few vegetables required for the afternoon's lunch, he waited, knowing that the good wife would open up soon.

The TV was running at full volume and he focused on the visuals but his wife was deep in thought. It was clear that her mind was not on the clamor. The back-and-forth between the journalists was heating up and they were targeting a prominent politician who was entangled in a shady deal that involved the taxpayer's money.

Ramakrishnan looked at his wife again. Anxiety enveloped her like a cloud. This had to stop. She would fall terribly sick. The man thought deeply for a moment and took a deep breath and walked over to the landline to complete the morning's unfinished conversation.

Pressing the redial button, he waited for his call to be picked up. This time, it was little Riya who spoke.

"Hello Riya, this is uncle Ramakrishnan. Can I speak to your mother? I hope she is not busy."

Sharada's heated stare was burning a hole in his back but he chose to disregard that. A decision had to be conveyed. They needed a change.

A few moments later Monika came on line and the two exchanged mutual pleasantries. A slight pause ensued soon after and Ramakrishnan took the opportunity of continuing with the conversation. They were advancing in years and needed the emotional support of good friends like her to ease out certain discomforts. So yes, they would accompany Monika's family after lunch. Sharada's famed sardine curry cooked in kokum and red chili paste was not to be wasted and he planned on having a hearty meal. They could all meet outside his house and have an enjoyable day out. Monika's husky laugh prompted a reluctant grin on Ramakrishnan's face and he turned to watch Sharada's expression.

                                                      Walk Away

Her pique dimmed and he relaxed. Sharada knew what her husband was trying to do. Well, the man had succeeded. Feeling lighter at heart, she switched off the offensive barrage and rose from her perch to make a beeline towards her workplace. Her husband would join her at the countertop and together, they would cook a handsome lunch.

Sharada washed, cleaned and definned the sardines while Ramakrishnan washed the kokum pieces. The couple worked in silence, well-accustomed to the process. Finicky Sharada was hard to please but he had mastered the art of surrender. Appeasement was the key to her happiness. Both knew each other well. She adored the man while he had grown to love this strong woman. Her intuitiveness complemented his gentleness. He was the balm to her soul. And she has given her all to ensure that he led a fulfilled life. Premediated actions borne out of a deep wish to offer everything that normalcy could do so at the drop of a hat. When a second pregnancy was deemed life threatening, she went all out confident that her Gods would not fail her. She would give her Ramakrishnan everything possible that money could not buy plus more.

Yet today, they were facing a tornado. The dark clouds were threatening to uproot all that she painstakingly built from scratch. What if her Rashi was not as subtle or resilient as her? The mother feared the worst. She would not dwell on what would happen rather, she focused on what best she could do. Pray.

Monika's offer was the salve that she has been unknowingly reaching out for. Ramakrishnan was right, as always. Today, they would beseech the all-powerful and entreat them for a beautiful soul's safe return. She picturized their daughter by their side, sitting on the counter top and languidly chewing on a piece of fruit.

"Rashi dear heart, come back to us soon. We are awaiting your presence by our side."

The cooking process was underway and Sharada worked mechanically. Her husband in the meantime, placed the kokum pieces in a small vessel and poured water over them so that the fruit was just covered. The water would soon turn dark and sour as it leached out its inherent flavor.

Sharada fired up the stove and place a well-used earthen pan over it. A few tablespoons of coconut oil was poured and as it began to smoke ever so lightly, she added mustard seeds, fenugreek seeds, slit green chilies, curry leaves, finely chopped ginger, crushed garlic, diced shallots, and once the mixture was thoroughly sautéed, half a teaspoon of turmeric powder, three heaped spoons of Kashmiri chili powder and the kokum pieces along with the water it was soaked in. As the mix began to boil, the sardines were dropped into the pan and allowed to cook for about ten to fifteen minutes. The stove was running on simmer mode all this while and Ramakrishnan hastened to lay the table. The previous day's yoghurt curry was warmed and placed on the table with a small pot of cooked rice, fried pappadams, and a bottle of homemade mango pickle. His senses were on high alert. The curry was his favorite and he would enjoy its flavorsome taste first. Sharada's worry would be set aside for a while as he feasted on the meen mulakittathe.* His gut told him that their daughter would be home soon. Neither God not demon would dare stand in this mother's way. When it came to fierce determination, his Sharada did not have an equal.

The stove had been switched off. He knew that the curry would be gently bubbling in the pot. The simmering concoction would now be garnished with a spoonful of coconut oil and a sprig of curry leaves. His mouth salivated in reaction. Sharada came out beaming; the still hot pan lay nestled within her fabric encased hands. His delight was ready to be served.

***

Palpable thoughts, an occasional tremor of the hands, sweat beading the upper lip, these were the only outward signs that revealed inner clamor. Vinay was oblivious to the signs. Dr. Priti instructed her husband to block the flight ticket for a Thursday afternoon. This would ensure that Rashi would be safe, well away from the demon that plagued her. It pained her to watch the degradation of a fine medical professional, a sensitive human being, who also happened to be her colleague. Fervent wishes for her colleague's safe travel ran on her lips these days. Money was not an issue. She would be repaid she knew. Rashi was someone who kept her word. But it was horrifying to take note of the sheer terror on her face every time their glances met. There was nothing she could say that would help lessen the strain. Two days to go. She dreaded the moment of reckoning and her husband wore a perpetually worried look which was quite unlike Dharmesh' normal demeanor.

Rashi was now on auto pilot mode. Her A.E had taken over. It was to be now or never.

Submission was easy. The rituals were a habit. Housework plus the additional demands were a routine thing. It helped while away the time. She reminded herself to dispose the birth control pills before she boarded the flight. They were not to be discovered. Her workbag could easily accommodate the camcorder, tapes and her passport. She would also carry her jacket with her. The internal drop in temperature was becoming harder to bear. Her teeth uncontrollably chattered and all that gnashing was making her jaw ache. Vinay noted her hunched posture only to enquire whether her monthly periods had been missed.

Seriously?

Inwardly her A.E. had burst out laughing. Rashi maintained the stoic demeanor with difficulty.

Did she glimpse hope in his eyes? The jerk. She felt revulsion at the thought.

A shudder coursed through her as she pictured the embrace that would have to be borne for the whole of today and, the night. This night.

"Lend me some strength Sharadamma. Help me be as wise as you. How right you were, to foresee the unimaginable and prod me relentlessly just so that I would pause to reflect, muster the courage and stop enduring," chanted her benumbed mind.

For this was fear that had seeped through all the pores of her body. The terror had wormed its way through, draining her of free thought. Both A.E. and Rashi had turned compliant, weak willed. It was Sharadamma's energy that was goading the dormant self to take charge, negotiate through the web it was encased in and take flight. Tomorrow would be now or never. If this failed, she would be a walking corpse, doomed to rot here, in this prison. Vinay's dominion over her would be complete.

6:30 a.m.

• Breakfast was to be readied.

• While Vinay showered, all the offensive materials had to be retrieved and stuffed inside the workbag earmarked for the purpose along with her passport and the strip of birth control pills. The duplicate key had to be secured within its snug hideaway; under her breast, held by the elastic band of her bra.

• Her jacket had to be retrieved off its hook as they left. This was an absolute must.

• Dishes to be cleared, shower, change and join Vinay in the car. The first 20 minutes would be most crucial. Dear God, please do not allow him to rifle through the contents of her bag.

In the shower, Rashi shivered as the warm water fell over her. The cold was increasingly becoming difficult to bear.

I miss you maa.

Tears fell unchecked and for a moment, she gave in.

The time. Look at the clock you idiot. Stop sniveling.

A.E's harsh reminder gave Rashi the control that was needed. Dressing up required a few minutes. After spraying on perfume, applying color to her lips and kohl to tired eyes that stared back, she joined the pallid faced monster at the door.

A.E.: The jacket, pick it up.

Vinay's, "Are you cold?" was deflected by a mute nod.

A.E.: She's not pregnant, you brainless oaf.

The man picked up her jacket and wordlessly draped it about her shoulders. She sensed A.E. flinch at the touch.

8:30 a.m.

And then they were out.

He drove slowly as though preoccupied.

Her insides clenched and unclenched as she watched the traffic mill around.

They finally reached her workplace. She climbed down from the massive SUV he loved. As he drove away, she felt a release. The chokehold grip on her emotions gradually wound down.

Fishing out her mobile from her purse, she dialed Priti's number, let it ring once and cut the call. Then, ever so calmly, she walked towards the reception where an unmarked envelope that contained her ticket to freedom and, a few dinars for her taxi ride and food expense awaited. What has she done to deserve such kindness, thought Rashi in wonder. It has to be her mother's love that was offering her protection. Sharadamma would know that she needed guidance. She would be at her altar, praying for her safety. Nothing was to go wrong now. She was at the threshold… almost.

Collecting the envelope from the receptionist, she turned quickly and walked outside the gate to hail a taxi to the airport.

***

Madan was driving a rented minivan towards the St. George Edapally church. It was Monika di's wish that they visit the *punyalan** first. The church that housed the Saint was an ancient one and had its origins pegged around 543 AD. Subsequent additions were added at a later stage. The imposing structure was a place where worshippers of all faiths visited chiefly to have their worries erased. The belief went that homes which had the occasional serpentine visitors, would see nothing of them once the believer prayed to the Saint. The reptiles would never surface within the walled perimeters of the faithful.

Another belief that was associated with the Saint's miraculous powers, was the fact that any property listed in the market that failed to attract potential buyers would see an instant reversal of fortune if a simple tip was followed. All the seller had to do, was to take a fistful of soil from the designated property/spot and place it within the house of worship and lo and behold, a sale would be instantly effectuated!

The Saint's benevolence extended to all who believed in his powers and Monika wanted both Sharadamma and Ramakrishnan to pray for their daughter's safety. In fact, Mala could be seen sitting cross legged on the floor of the van, looking out in silent contemplation. Perhaps she has already begun her prayers. Pritam steadied the effervescent twins as the group approached the church premises. Madan parked their vehicle under the shade of a tree. The setting sun cast a glow and the group walked on towards the façade of the church. Scores of devotees milled about while some had already completed their musings and prepared to exit the scene.

The group entered the wide hall that was flanked by tall carved doors and sat on long wooden seats for the best part of an hour. Madan and Pritam ushered the twins outside as they were beginning to get out of hand. The foursome strolled about the grounds and stood watching a pond that teemed with fishes. The grounds that the structure stood on was huge and it shared space with a powerful neighbor - the Kottaram Ganapathy temple. Local lore states that a compound wall once built to separate the adjacent grounds crumbled away. When this happened a couple of times, the people simply gave up and accepted the verdict that was conveyed by an unseen hand.

Ganapathy or, Ganesha is the elephant headed God of the Hindus, son of Shiva-Parvathy and brother to Subramaniam and Iyyapan. He is known to be the one who clears all obstacles that his devotees face and this temple in particular has its doors open to the general public from five to seven thirty in the morning and, seven to ten in the evening. An early morning slot is reserved for the rituals conducted by members and benefactors of the Edapally Royal family under whose aegis remains the temple.

It is to be noted here that the idol of the Lord remains visible to the general public but those of his family members that surround him within the sanctum sanctorum, are hidden from view. This is supposedly a rare occurrence and devotees swear by the miracles that abound, some of the tales now being part of the local lore along with the mythical quality attributed to the divine Lord.

After the customary circumambulation of the perimeter of the temple, the group walked in the direction of their parked vehicle, much lighter at heart. Except for the frolicking twins, each and every one prayed for Rashi's well-being. She was dear to all of them. Right from the time she has pranced around, hair bunched in two ponytails

Walk Away

to her advancement as a medical professional and her wedding that had been the talk of the town, Rashi had dazzled all with her beauty and graciousness. What exactly had gone wrong was a mystery and none had the heart to question the aged couple. Yet, each member of the close-knit group prayed fervently for the loving Sharadamma and kind-hearted Ramakrishnan's for their prayers to be answered. Their lives had been touched by the two for as long as they could remember and it was time they offered support in whatever way possible.

Monika, Pritam, Mala and Madan wanted the heavens to listen to their collective prayers. And when the heavens did respond, they would be ready and waiting.

***

9:45 a.m.

Rashi alighted from her cab in front of the gleaming Bahrain International airport. She looked at her watch and sighed in relief. Paying the cabbie his fare, she walked towards the gate marked 'Departure.' The place looked deserted. The lack of a crowd was a relief. She did not want to be targeted by aunties and harried mothers travelling with their infants or wailing kids. The lack of baggage would stir curiosity among such women and that, was something she had to avoid at any cost.

The ticket counter was manned by a gracious young man who noted her lack of luggage without comment and proceeded to enter her details with calm efficiency. Vinay had conveniently forgotten to mention that he would travel to the nearby emirate that day but Rashi knew his schedule well. Moreover, he belonged to a department that worked behind the scenes so there was no worry of a slip up. The front-end personnel would not recognize him unless they ran a detailed check.

Rashi collected her boarding pass and walked towards the immigration checkpoint. After being body scanned, she collected her handbag and walked over to the Duty-Free section for a bit of window shopping. There were so many things she longed for. Perfumes, chocolates, a liquor bottle for Pritam and Monika in fact, there was an offer for it today *damn her luck*. The branded handbags lured her and she inspected a few tags. Walking over to an upright stand that was stacked with books and magazines, Rashi rifled through a few of them. A jewelry ad caught her attention and she froze. She had missed out on something. Her carefully executed plan was in fact, incomplete and she could not leave now. It was her trousseau - the jewelry that was gifted to her by her parents and secured in a bank vault that was operated by the D. The collection had been painstakingly assembled by her parents over the years in anticipation of her special day. She remembered episodes wherein the money for each set was paid in instalments and handled lovingly before they were returned to their beautiful boxes and stored until the time came for them to be given away to the bride and groom. Over a kilo of gold and assorted gemstones that was secured within the confines of Vinay's bank locker to which, he had the key.

Another key to be retrieved.

She had to turn back.

This journey would be incomplete if she gifted the very thing her parents had painstakingly amassed over the years to the demon. She was not worried about the money she had earned and would soon lose. That was inconsequential. But the gold; the valuable gift her parents bequeathed her, was proof of their love. She would not spurn that just to get away from the devil.

Rashi picked out a few dinars from her bag and purchased a phone calling card from the counter. Walking up to the row of phones that were placed on the opposite wall, she dialed the number that was engraved in her heart.

"Hello."

The answering call broke Rashi's heart. It has been so long. One long heart wrenching moment passed.

Sharadamma knew. This was her Rashi. She waited with bated breath as her fingers clasped the receiver of the phone tightly.

"Talk to me my daughter."

"Amma…" One word.

The air was loaded with emotions.

"I'm in the airport..." Sharadamma sucked in her breath. The elation threatened to overwhelm.

"...but I need to go back. There's something I must do." Rashi heaved in anguish as she spoke but she fought for control.

"Give me a weeks' time and I'll be there. Tell Dad not to worry. I'll need his help as soon as I touchdown. I'll call you... pray for me amma. One week."

The phone went silent.

Rashi walked to the restroom, entered a cubicle, bolted the door, and sobbed her heart out.

Sharadamma replaced the receiver of the phone mutely and walked towards the backyard where her husband was tending to the plants. They needed to be alert. They had to be ready.

A good fifteen minutes later, Rashi walked out of the washroom, composed. She exited the Duty-free area, re-entered the immigration lounge and politely informed the staff that she had to go back. There was an emergency at her workplace. She took the escalator that went down to the first floor and walked out of the doors into the bright blazing sun.

11:00 a.m. the same day

Rashi got down from the prepaid taxi in front of her workplace, paid the cabdriver and entered the hospital premises.

She went up to her friend's room. Priti had promised to hold fort for the day. Rashi's absence would not be missed until she received her call from home base. Her consternation was great when she saw her friend entering her room. Rashi explained to her how and why she had turned back and insisted that she had not missed out on the chance of a lifetime. Priti had been dumbfounded at first, wild with anger afterwards. The flight could have been easily boarded. Their careful planning had all been for nothing.

Rashi looked her in the eye.

"This is something I need to do Doc. This is my integrity on the line. Everything that I stand for. I cannot bear to have it stolen from me. I need to do this. Please understand my plight."

Her plea touched someplace deep and Priti found herself relenting.

She extended her hand in mute enquiry and Rashi handed out the boarding pass and tickets to her. Dr. Priti proceeded to tear them into tiny pieces and flushed them down the toilet bowl. The episode would be consigned to their memory for now. Until the time, the next opportunity presented itself, they would wait and watch. Both women had shed their cloaks of uncertainty and garbed the mantle of efficient professionals. This was only a trial run. When the right time presented itself, they could effortlessly cover the pace; it would take about a week for everything to fall into place.

***

The demon was feeling odd of late. Rashi seemed restless. Her furtive looks convinced him that something was amiss. There were tremors that wracked her body and she shivered from its ill effects. His mother's offhand remark that her daughter-in-law could be pregnant set him thinking. He had tried his best to plant his offshoot within her but in vain. If his mother was right, he would be the happiest man on earth. Perhaps women displayed weird mannerisms when their bodies began to change. It was funny he thought, that his loving gestures did not seem distasteful to her of late. Maybe she was changing. She had begun to sense his affection towards her. Her eyes emitted a gleam nowadays. He could not pinpoint the true nature of those glances but they satisfied him. Her earlier evasiveness drove him up the wall. She was his wife for heaven's sake not some chattel he picked up from the streets. Did she not understand that he truly loved her? It was true that when she refused to respond he would lose his cool, and retaliate. The shame and reproach would cloud him once he calmed down. But it was not his fault, was it? His mother told him that women were meant to accept the dominion of the male gender. His future wife would have to adjust and accept his whims and fancies. After all they were bound to stay together forever. Vinay smiled in glee. His insides stirred as he pan fried a whole pomfret in a frypan. There were two more of them, neatly stacked on paper towels in a plate placed beside the stove. Slices of lemon and onion rings were arranged around the fried marvel. Vinay admired his handiwork. His appetite was rising.

Rashi in the meantime, had completed her shower and was relaxing in front of the television. Their evenings almost always ended this way. He cooked dinner for the two with the help of recipes jotted down in a notebook that were his mother-in-law's secret ammunition for a happy and satisfactory family life. He pictured the fun they would have soon after and his chin trembled. The anticipation in him rose to a fervent pitch. He prayed that his wife would cooperate and not earn his wrath. Things would only get out of hand and he would bitterly regret his actions the next morning. He hated Rashi for provoking him. Hadn't she been schooled by her 'shrewd' mother that a husband was to be pleased in the manner befitting him and non-capitulation was considered an act of folly?

He remembered smashing her phone in anger and usurping her ATM card on one occasion when she had threatened to walk out on him. The gall. She had the nerve to talk back to him. The fool. Did she think that she was the man of the house? Well, she would not have a penny of what she earned if that was the reason for her arrogance. And she would not be allowed to consult with her mother as per his mother's advice. And things had gone well after that. His Rashi had submitted. Capitulated without a murmur. She knew that he had her best interests at heart, mulled Vinay with a smile as he carried the plates of rice, eggplant curry and fried fish to the dining table. Rashi would join him with a pleased smile. She loved well cooked food. And the secret to her heart were the recipes that turned out perfect dishes, same as her mother. Vinay believed that he held the keys to her heart. Of late he had come to the realization that she had truly become his. The two ate in silence, each absorbed in his/her thoughts. One was ecstatic while the other was mired in abject gloom. Later, as they lay exhausted in bed, Vinay remarked casually, "Rashi, I have decided to take an off tomorrow."

Rashi's heart sank. Had he discovered something? She suddenly felt nauseous. Her stomach heaved in protest and she scrambled towards the bathroom. Vinay settled against the pillows with a satisfied smile. This was an encouraging sign. A new member was on the way. His spirits lifted further and he felt the heady rush that indicated another exciting half an hour with his ever-obliging wife. He waited for the sounds to cease and for his wife to wriggle in between the cool covers. Vinay reached out for her.

There was to be no respite from the assault, mocked A.E.

Expect neither tenderness nor mercy from this one. Wait for the right opportunity Rashi. Bide your time.

This time, the devil dozed off almost immediately. He was spent, sated. Rashi sat on the bed and grunted in pain. She hurt all over. Wincing, she moved and her feet touched the icy floor. A sudden blast of cold air hit her body as the covers slipped off. Rashi walked towards the window and peeked at the glinting moon from between the curtains. She ached to be free of this gilded cage. She wished for a happy, torment-free life. What use was her body when her soul craved for escape? Of what use was her education when she couldn't save herself from vile moments such as this? She was being used over and over again under the guise of a license – the one that proclaimed her marital status to the whole world. This could be a result of the curse meted out to her by Sahaj. Poor Sahaj worshipped the very ground she walked upon. He adored her and gazed at her with 'that' look in his eyes. Her photo nestled in a pocket next to his heart. He has been so disappointed by the news of her engagement that he had fled… fled from the milling crowd that surrounded them; heartbroken, never to be seen by anyone in and around the area.

Rashi sighed as a tear slipped from her cheek and trailed a lonely path downwards. Karma was a bitch, it was rightly said. She was undergoing the trauma in bits until she felt the agony ripple and pierce her heart. The shear was slow but cut deep until she could bleed no more.

This had to stop. The agony had to cease. It was either that, or something far more terrible that would meander in and the very thought paralyzed her. Wondering what was in store for her the next day, Rashi walked into the bathroom, turned on the faucet and allowed the warm water to soothe her.

***

        Walk Away

Mala grew anxious as days that were grim and filled with foreboding passed by. Rashi was like her daughter. There were many a time when her children had bonded and interacted with the well-behaved girl. Once the veil of dissatisfaction and anger lifted from the girl's heart, she had turned into a demure and sweet person. Her mother had turned more patient and kind-hearted in dealing with her and even Madan had remarked on the change in relationship. Her son Madan was equally responsible and worked hard to give them a good life.

Prasad was a weakling and a wastrel right from the beginning and her children knew that they owed their mother everything. Yet, their father could not be abandoned. He was like the one spoke in their wheel that did not offer anything by way of support and yet, could not be discarded. His presence was silent, invisible and like a shadow. They did not need him but were secretly relieved that the position that he occupied within the family remained steady. The grandchildren doted on him. He was mild mannered and affectionate to their demands. Sheru was the only one who could keep him leashed. The man quailed before the boy's fierceness, she thought in amusement.

Of course, Monika di and Sharadamma had been her mainstay since the time they had fled from Mumbai. Monika di faced terrible days too. Those days were behind them and they were now in good hands. And now this. What evil was the girl facing? How could they help her? Mala's anxiousness resurfaced and she began to chant the Hanuman Chalisa*. The prayer beads rolled and dipped gently as her fingers moved over them and stilled as she prayed. Hanumanji* could root out the worst of evils from a person's life. He had helped her tide over countless worries.

How could a miniscule tremor rock their boat when he looked out for them? Her devotion for the eternal Brahmachari* and worshipper of Lord Rama, who was blessed by ShaniDev and could thus revert the ill effects of the present into something fortuitous was steadfast. Rashi had suffered but she would soon be in their midst. The vapors would lift soon and allow fresh air to take its place.

Monika rolled up her yoga mat, watered her plants, and was busy in the kitchen cooking up a storm. She needed to be with her dear friends at the Pallikal house. Their visit to the St. George Edapally church and the Kottaram Ganapathy temple calmed her heart. It has been a good outing… something, that was meant to be. Sharada aunty seemed happier after their trip. Perhaps the storm in her heart had quelled.

Pritam took them to a local shack afterwards. Its entrance faced the sea and they all sat at the long table looking towards the waves that rose and fell.

The children had steaming bowls of a seafood soup placed before them. Then there was *neyy chchoru* (ghee rice) and crab curry followed by *aykora pollichath* - pearl spot slathered in a flavorful paste; wrapped in banana leaves and steamed, boiled eggs in coconut gravy and *noolputtu* (stringhoppers). The conversation level had been minimal and the food was attacked with gusto. Perhaps relief helped make inroads and the feeling of dread had lessened. Once the plates were cleared and cups of milky tea passed around, light chatter ensued. Pritam spoke at length about his work and Monika described her day at home with the kids.

Madan interjected at length about his job, the shifts and the interns who occupied his vehicle. They almost always slept through the journey regardless of the time. Conversations were minimal as most were fixated on their smartphones. The job was demanding and monotonous but it paid well and kept his family going. Nobody talked or laughed anymore, he reflected. Nothing seemed to amuse the new generation, inured as they were to the screens and the entertainment it offered them. Interactions and eye level contact was a thing of the past. Certain actions were habituated - a thank you, was said out of habit.

The emotional connect to such phrases were absent. Smiles were laced with artifice. The essence of naturality had been robbed from them. It hurt sometimes to note that a request was conveyed with a gruffness and without empathy. Something was ebbing out of humanity. Perhaps the city-life was to be blamed? The people from his mother's village seemed content, inviting and happier. They were respectful of who you were and how you responded to each other as a unit. Today's meet reminded him of that, the connect they shared. They had a common bond and that, made them a family.

Madan's talk soothed the senses. This was the talk of a common man. They shared an inherent trait and were proud of it. It was the empathy that brought them all together. Rashi was part of that circle and they would envelop her in its warmth. Sharada and Ramakrishnan felt reassured. They had nothing to worry about.

Afterwards, the group collected themselves and walked towards the waves, their feet rising and sinking through the grains of sand as the setting sun lent an orange sheen to the sky and a gentle wind blew softly around them. Riya and Siya shrieked and ran towards the waves while Pritam and Madan struggled to match their exuberance. Monika and Mala sat by Sharada's side while Ramakrishnan preferred to stand. The group stayed silent with each absorbed in their thoughts. When would Rashi be back. Most importantly, how soon?

***

Rashi had a sudden craving for food that offered comfort - her mother's *uruttu chammandi* mixed with hot rice for instance. This was something she could blitz through in an instant. The ingredients were all ready and available at home. All that was required, was a quick churn in the blender. Of course, when ground using a rounded pestle over a flat stone surface that had its face worn smooth from years of use, the flavors that exploded as one took in a mouthful was nothing compared to the concoction created using modern appliances. The coarsely ground mix was scooped out and shaped into a rough, round ball. The word 'uruttu' literally meant the same - being shaped. So, she peeled the skin off a few red onions, added some chopped ginger, a few curry leaves, a micro sized piece of tamarind, salt to taste, a few dry red chilies, a quarter spoon of Kashmiri chili powder and the ingredients were topped with half a cup of grated coconut. The blender pulsed to life and the mix was inspected. The chilies stood upright and a few whole shallots had come up to the surface so she gave the mixture a toss, closed the jar and gave the jar a quick shake. This time the ingredients settled down and the blender was once again given a quick pulse. The rough mix was scooped and gently molded into a round shape that sat snug in the palm of her hand. Rashi pinched out a minute sample from the *chammandi* and savored the taste. It was spicy, tangy and her taste buds trilled in happiness. This was rustic Kerala on a plate. Ecstasy whipped and served in under five minutes. The beauty of the combined flavors was such that, a simple plate of rice gruel or steamed rice would turn into the perfect accomplishment. Truly, this was a masterful invention. A simple, non-fussy recipe that was designed to enrich your palate and lift your mood in an instant.

Vinay entered the kitchen and promptly turned up his nose. Well, he could rot away, though Rashi. He had his eyes glued on Sharadamma's bone broth recipe. She felt like snatching the book from under his nose. Didn't his mother cook? Or didn't she have a few tricks up her sleeve that she could teach her son? Perhaps, they only knew how to take. They expected to be served and in return, what had been offered was one hell of a gift. She had endured them for so long and time had come for them to be repaid in kind. Oh, she was not the vengeful kind. Rather, she was the one to step away. And for that to happen, the Lord above needed to shine his light on her. She was running out of time.

"What are you thinking?" enquired her husband in his deceptively dulcet tone.

Rashi was roused from her reverie rather suddenly. Glancing at him, she shrugged her shoulders in reply and walked out of the space that they shared. Being this close to him was claustrophobic. She would wash and dress herself. He could relax at home for all she cared.

"Since I'm at home, we could visit your doctor friend at the hospital. What say?" Rashi froze in terror. This was a potential landmine that could go off in an instant.

"You need to get checked. Looking peaky off-late. Perhaps you have a condition?" the gloat was pretty evident in the voice.

Rashi shook like a leaf. What could be done? The idiot actually thought that he was going to be a father. Priti's gentle face rose unbidden into her thoughts. The good doctor would find a way out of her predicament, she reassured herself. This was not a do-or-die situation. They had to tip-toe their way out of this, unscathed that is.

An hour later, Vinay walked into her workplace with a self-conscious Rashi by his side. The stares were surreptitious. She hoped that no one would walk up to them and ask for a formal introduction. The normality of the act would set her teeth at edge. Vinay on the other hand would enjoy the attention. The cuckold strutted ahead as though he owned the place. When they neared the lift, he looked around for her and she quickly stepped in front and entered it. The sooner this charade was over, the better. Pressing the button for the fourth floor, she prayed frantically for her friend to be available. It would be a slow and painful evening one, that might even result in her death. And she wished to reach home in one piece. Her limp was a grim reminder of days spent in sheer terror with not a person who could be trusted with her secret. Turning to the right after stepping off the lift, she nodded at the faces who smiled at her in greeting. The nurse at the station confirmed that Doctor Priti was on call and she could slip in after the current patient left. Vinay abhorred the antiseptic smell of hospitals and she could feel him trying to hold his breath. She suppressed the chuckle that threatened to burst out and composed herself.

The gynae ward of the hospital was one of the busiest sections in the entire block. Nurses and physicians milled around and patients waited in the areas allotted to them. There were technicians and ward boys jostling about and the entire operation functioned like a well-oiled machine. Rashi noticed the elderly Mrs. Mittal waiting with her heavily pregnant mother-in-law. She walked over to them and exchanged pleasantries conscious of the gaze that was trained on her. Ignoring the unpleasant sensation, she continued the conversation. She was expected to sit by his side like the docile wife she was meant to be but deep within her, the tide had changed. A day or two of keeping up with this pretense and hopefully, she could relax. When Priti herself came out to receive them, Vinay was pleased. Rashi had taken care to register her name alongside her husband's so that the good Doctor would be alerted.

The duo entered the room and Vinay chatted amicably with the Doctor. Both Rashi and Dr. Priti knew what was coming. Yet, for a moment the suddenness of it threw the Doctor off guard.

"My wife has been looking rather pale and off color recently. My mother thinks that a baby is on the way. I wanted to discuss this with you in personal which is why, I took an off today. Nothing could be more important to me than this Doctor."

Not even the welfare of your wife, you dimwit? Dr. Priti ranted inwardly. Clearing her throat and turning to look at Rashi, she queried, "Are you late? Have you tested yourself at home?"

Rashi nodded a 'yes' to the first and a 'no' to the second question. Vinay grunted in irritation. "Let's draw a blood sample and get yourself checked. You could be anemic for all I know."

Turning to Vinay she asked, "Has she been eating well lately?"

"Of course. I'm the one who cooks at home. She does nothing at home except watch TV."

And cater to your incessant demands. Which woman would have the strength to complete the household chores after all the rigor, you creep?

"I'll write out some iron tabs plus a fortifying tonic for Rashi. The results of the test might take time… two days perhaps." This was a lie. Normally, it took less than a day.

Rashi stole a look at Priti who was listing out a series of steps with a deadpan face. Vinay tried to look interested but Rashi knew that his patience was wearing thin. Irritation radiated from his physique like a cloud. She let them continue and looked out of the window. The grey exterior of the neighboring building suddenly seemed interesting. She had to speed up with her planning. Things might get out of hand. The hag would certainly work on her son's mind in her dulcet tone. And that would be the end of her. His acute disappointment would override whatever reasoning powers circulated within his small brain and devastate her forever.

Rashi caught the Doctor's eye and a momentary message was conveyed.

They.had.to.speed.up.

The second key had to be duplicated. Dharmesh had to deliver in double-quick time and she would have to accelerate her actions. The first time had been a rehearsal and she thanked God for it. Beside her, Vinay vibrated like an animal in heat. Dissatisfaction emanated from his person in waves and she began to feel mortally afraid. Her tongue seemed to be glued to the top of her mouth.

Dr. Priti indicated that Vinay was to wait outside while Rashi had her blood drawn. Once he was out of earshot, she pressed Rashi's arm in sympathy and offered her a glass of water. The terror she had detected in the poor girl's eyes was real.

***

Ammu's narration had wound to a stop.

The painful memories were one too many and I (Vinitha) did not want her to relive the agony.

I was told at a later date that her flight to freedom had been successful the second time around. That she had reached her destination was obvious. I was sitting in front of her and coming to grips with her story. Her demons were my demons. I felt her inner pain and the numbness wash over me. Felt the relief clear away everything that had been endured, the minute the aircraft took off.

Ramakrishnan had waited for his daughter to disembark and they had rushed to the bank to retrieve her jewelry from the locker. The action was important enough to her although it mattered least to her parents. They wanted her safe, in their midst. What did they care for the material things that were associated with their precious first-born? However, Rashi's insistence that not a second was to be wasted for the formalities to be completed was to be considered. She knew that the bank manager would inform the D of the latest development. It was therefore imperative that the precious valuables her parents had painstakingly collected to ensure her happiness, was to be cleared out right that instant. The rest, he could bake, boil, steam and stuff down his gullet for all she cared.

Dr. Priti was wired the money that was due. The family owed her and Dharmesh their very existence. Sharadamma offered her blessings to the couple every single day until the time she departed from the physical world. She had stayed on long enough to watch Rashi turn into her new avatar. Perhaps she had intended that Ammu enter my orbit and for loyal Ajin to stay by her side. As for her story - Ammu was insistent that it be heard; by all the Ammu's out there who required a boost in morale. The ones that needed to understand that hope is but a heartbeat away.

It takes courage to walk out or, walk away, pick the pieces and rebuild. Starting all over again is tough but giving up is never the answer. The life we are given, is to be used to the fullest. The days ahead of us, are to be redeemed and explored. Newer experiences are lessons that are to be enjoyed. Despair is to give up… to lose. And that is something that does not exist in the Ammu I know. The key takeaway through her personal journey is the realization that there is so much more to us than what meets the eye. In her words:

"It took me five years to get a day's worth of serenity. The right moment to walk away seemed to be a distant dream - 547 days of torment endured at the hands of a sadist who possessed the license to inflict torment. That I was able to flee, speaks volumes of the faith my loved ones had in me. Else, I would not be here before you narrating my story. Heaven knows how many like me suffer agony at the hands of their partners. I shudder to think what would have happened had I failed in my escape attempt. Perhaps I would have been mercilessly slaughtered and he would have gotten away with that as well. Being financially secure is a formidable weapon in a man and when wielded, none dare oppose his view or actions.

The world is evolving they say, but I am yet to see it. For, thoughts are the key. And if that doesn't change, nothing will."

Ammu has taught me so much. In fact, she continues to impart crucial life lessons every other day.

The metamorphosis is never really complete. If we understand this, then all will be well.

***

GLOSSARY

Abbakka Chowta - Abbakka Rani was the queen of Tulunadu who fought the Portuguese in the latter half of the 16th century. Abbakka's memory is much cherished in her home town of Ullal which is a part of modern Mangalore. The 'Veera Rani Abbakka Utsava' is an annual celebration held in her memory.

Anganwadi - Anganwadi is a type of rural child care center in India. They were started by the Indian government in 1975 as part of the Integrated Child Development Services program to combat child hunger and malnutrition. Anganwadi means 'courtyard shelter' in Hindi.

Bai - A common colloquial phrase used for a lady house-help in Mumbai.

Bhaiyya - Brother in Hindi.

Bhikari - Seeker of alms.

'Bol yaar. Mein tere liye kya kar sakti hoon?' - Tell me my friend, how can I help you? (Hindi)

Brahmachari - A bachelor.

'Chalega?' - Is it fine with you?

Dabba - Storage box.

Didi - Sister.

Guruji/Swamiji - Revered teacher.

Hanumanji - The revered Monkey God, Hanuman.

Hanuman Chalisa - Saint Tulsidas wrote the devotional hymn in praise of Lord Hanuman in the 15th century.

Jhadoo - Broom.

Kholi - is a Marathi word that means 'room' or, 'place of stay.'

Mahadev - One among several terms that is used to address Lord Shiva.

Maharani - Queen.

Malkin - The lady of the house.

Mamay - A colloquial term used to address a dear friend.

Mambazha pulissery - A yoghurt-based dish of Kerala that has ripe mangoes as its chief ingredient.

Mandaram - The Bauhinia Acuminata is a species of flowering shrub native to tropical southeastern Asia. In Kerala, it is used as an offering to Lord Shiva.

Matoshri - Revered Mother.

Meen mulakittathe - A traditional fish curry of Kerala which involves the use of kokum and other spices.

Namaste - The traditional Indian way of greeting the opposite person or group.

Neyy chchoru - Ghee rice of the south as opposed to the pulav of the north. The south Indian version is milder in flavor and uses other versions of the grain as opposed to basmati rice.

Nithya Kalyani - Periwinkle flower.

Orey - Hey you!

Pappadam - A seasoned flatbread made out of black gram bean flour and is either fried in oil or baked under dry heat until crunchy.

Pavitra Savitri - A pure and pious woman.

Punyalan - Saint.

Pujya - A respectful form of address of a person of stature.

Rasmalai - A milk based sweet.

Saho - A colloquial term used to address a dear friend.

Sandaas - A Hindi term for restroom.

Shoorpanakha - Sister of the Asura king Ravana.

Sulaimani -Black tea with or without sugar and spiced with a tinge of lemon.

Taluk - District.

www.ingramcontent.com/pod-product-compliance
Lightning Source LLC
Chambersburg PA
CBHW020454180726
47992CB00027B/2333